To Hold Back the Dark

EVELYN RAINEY

Paperback ISBN-13: 978- 978-1-946469-28-1

Sheltering Tree.Earth, LLC Publishing
PO Box 973, Eagle Lake, FL 33839

http://ShelteringTree.Earth

DEDICATION

I would like to dedicate this book to all the wonderful hospice CNAs, Nurse Rachel, Chaplain Jeff, and social worker Roz who take care of my mother. I especially want to include her daily CNA Tif in this dedication. You all spend your talents and life **holding back the dark**. Thank you.

CONTENTS

PREVIOUSLY

There is a war between good and evil that rages through the universe. The objective of those who serve the Dark is to turn as many to the dark as they can. The objective of those who serve the Light is to kill swiftly and mercifully those who serve the Dark, so as not to inflict torture or perpetuate despair.

When someone prays intensely, the energy opens a portal of light. Conversely, when a great evil is done, the energy opens a door of despair. Only someone who serves the Light can go through a portal. Only those who serve the Dark can go through a door. Portals of light and doors of despair have been opening on worlds for eternity; one of those worlds is Earth.

Comes the Warrior

The Angel of the Lord warned Reverend Atticus Jordan that the war was coming to Earth, but a warrior would be sent to him to help train an army to hold back the dark. The angel neglected to tell Atticus that Gwen, the warrior, would be pregnant and may not want to fight anymore.

Each elder in Atticus' church has faced despair – death, loss, betrayal -- and chosen to live in hope, joy, and grace. They know that the war is coming; they know that they must choose again, for Light or Dark, when Gwen shows up at Morning Creek.

Roving bands of looters in black capes and swords catch the attention of Colonel Morgan Forest of the Internal Intelligence Agency who has fought wars his entire life. His trail leads him to Gwen, and Gwen's trail leads him to this radical band of parishioners. He sends in his spy; he knows they have formed a militia. He could stop them; he could destroy their sect with a stroke of his pen. But for Morgan, the shadow-line between darkness and light is not that precise.

To Build an Army

Atticus and his Church of Refuge, forewarned by the Angel of the Lord, is preparing to hold back the Dark that is expanding across the worlds. Prayer, staffs, swords, martial arts – all are brave tools in the hands of the Lambs of Light. But the war fought by those who serve the Light, the Bringers of Light, and the Light Eternal is not limited to humans, it encompasses all creatures which have souls.

"Atticus."

When the six-year-old opened his eyes to the voice, his bedroom was filled with light.

"Atticus, wake up."

Atticus sat up and rubbed his eyes. "Who are you?"

"You know me, Atticus. You must hurry."

"I know you? Who are you?" He tried to see into the white light.

"Atticus, I have known you all of my life. Trust me. Trust me now or it will all be for nothing. Get under your bed."

"Do what?"

"Get under your bed, Atticus."

Atticus shrugged and then stood up. As the six-year-old crawled under his bed, the window in his room shattered and gun fire riddled holes into where he had been sleeping.

1 QUEEN VENUTHA

"Mom, tell Dad I am, TOO, going with him to see Otka's dragons!" Venutha's command could be heard by the Horsemen of Atticus as they walked onto the mess hall's front porch.

Ben's retort was just as loud. "Joan, tell my daughter she is NOT going with me!"

The horsemen paused at the double doors and exchanged grins.

Jeremy put his hand on the door, "This morning's muck chores says Venutha gets to go."

"Boy," Wren-at-Dawn laughed, "The day the queen doesn't get her way with Ben is the day I will muck all the stables by myself."

The Horsemen of Atticus chuckled and walked into the mess hall for breakfast.

The Jamaican Me Hungry Hall was large enough to seat fifty with benches and tables scattered around in a friendly way. The three dozen horsemen and dog guards, along with Ben's family, sat here for most of their meals. But anyone was welcome. The cooks and staff were refugees from other worlds, like most of the horsemen. But they were like family, too, and the morning was filled with the smell of wonderful food and the sound of friendship.

Venutha the Queen stood off to the side, hands on hips, bull-dog tenacity on her face. She was dressed in faux leather leggings, cuffed ankle boots, short broomstick skirt in geometric turquoise and terracotta and gold, a peasant blouse that looked useless over her flat chest, beaded hoop earring, and sterling rings on every finger. Ugly ducklings are supposed to magically transform into gracious swans with time. That hadn't happened to Venutha yet.

Ben, in jeans, plaid flannel shirt and a red face, also had his hands on his hips.

Joan, Ben's wife and Venutha's adopted mother sat on a bench beside a high chair, spooning oatmeal into Baby Ben's mouth. Her stomach was swollen with five months of pregnancy. Her face was the very picture of contentment. A slight smile lifted one corner of her mouth as she ignored her husband and daughter.

Pierre hobbled over to them, leaning heavily on his cane. His right knee had shattered in a parachute landing during Operation Iraqi Freedom fifteen years earlier, but what little stability the fused bones had given him were negated by a blow from the staff of a dark soldier two years ago as he and his horses fought to hold back the dark on Ganternon. Wren-at-Dawn walked beside him, carrying a tray loaded with both men's breakfasts.

Hreno made a little screech of joy and jumped up from her table to tackle two people in hugs: Mitchell and Shadow. Mitchell, Wren-at-Dawn, and Hreno first met Shadow five years ago during the Battle of Crystal Lake. Shadow had been the weave of Lord Marcelux, but escaped during the battle and now lived in Mitchell's dorm. The two were always together. But Hreno joined them as often as she could. The young man was thick with latent muscles under a layer of softness. His tanned face and jet black curls were average. His eyes set him apart. He never seemed to see what was in front of him, but what lay beyond now and here. He was a weave without a redeemer. Hreno and Shadow often whispered fearfully that he was in danger of losing himself to the Weave, so they stayed close by whenever he opened a portal.

Distracted from her brewing tirade, Venutha smiled and went to join her friends. "What are you doing here this early?"

3

"We're weaving the portal for your father and Pierre." The blind girl embraced Venutha.

"They get to go?" Venutha shrieked over her shoulder.

Ben curled his shoulders, his back to her, and continued his breakfast.

Venutha loved the sound her new boots made as she stomped back to his table. "Why do they get to go and I don't?"

Wren-at-Dawn whistled twice and counted with his fingers raised above his head: one, two, three. The hall resounded as everyone present shouted, "It's not fair!"

Venutha punched Wren's shoulder. He rolled his gorgeous brown eyes at her and smiled.

"We're not going through to Risardia, we're just weaving the portal." Shadow sat beside Hreno.

Venutha stomped her new boots out of the mess hall and across the wooden porch.

Ben sighed in utter relief. His wife leaned toward him while wiping oatmeal from Baby Ben's fingers, "I'm proud of you. You did a good job of letting her throw her tantrum and just taking those deep breaths."

"You did good, partner," Pierre patted his arm.

Jeremy raised his voice from two tables away, "Guess we know who's mucking the stables today."

Wren-at-Dawn rubbed the back of his fingers along his chestnut beard and nodded. "Tell Atticus a miracle has happened at the Ranch."

Ben blinked and reddened. Joan beamed with pride.

2 A WAILING COUNTRY SONG

"You'll like it here, Mom," Gabriel Iglesias lifted his mother-in-law's bags out of the trunk and headed with her into the house. "There's people from all over, really all over, but everyone speaks the same language. And there's almost no crime ever. I mean, there may be a car accident, or a fist-fight, but no theft and no murders in almost seven years."

"So you're getting paid for doing nothing."

The sheriff of Morning Creek County cringed at the tone of her voice, but shrugged it off as transferred grief. His wife's father had just died, leaving Debbie with an upside-down mortgage, a dozen maxed credit cards, and the legend of being a womanizer three counties-wide. To Iglesias, Debbie was the epitome of a wailing country song. She'd fallen for the first cowboy who looked her way, went to church every Sunday and Wednesday, raised three girls with a firm but loving hand, and stood by her man, loving him almost beyond reason.

Gabriel's wife Becky hugged Debbie, as did their two sons, Devon and Thomas. His boys, ten and eight, loved living in Morning Creek. They'd moved here four years ago, when the previous sheriff Joan Peters got married to the local veterinarian Ben Feinstein and resigned. Colonel Morgan Forest of the IIA approached him with the job offer. The IIA had nothing to do with hiring sheriffs anywhere else in the US. Just here, at Morning Creek, with the Church of the Refuge and the Ranch and the Rutger Perkins Hospital, secretly renown for curing the incurable. Most people had never heard of Morning Creek; but Gabriel had fought in the Battle of Crystal Lake five years ago. When Morgan offered him the position, Gabriel didn't hesitate to accept.

3 THE REFUGE

Atticus had been toying with the idea of using the Tower of Babel as a sermon. He always liked that story as a child – now he knew it was a creation myth – but still – the science fiction of his current life matched well with the old story. He sighed and turned away from his laptop – the words just wouldn't flow. Atticus looked out of his office window to the compound below.

Three thousand children and hundreds of adults formed organized clusters according to their weapon of choice. Doug led two hundred Hands through exercises designed to quickly and efficiently incapacitate the enemy. Tyler led the Fingers and Toes in defensive moves. Tyler's wife Ricean led her Swords through what looked like a ballet. Taralyn, Doug's wife and Tyler's daughter, was too far along in her pregnancy to physically lead her Staffs, so she gave instructions from the side lines, shouting encouragements and scolding with equal vigor. The sound of musical instruments swelled from inside the sanctuary as Eduviges McGuinna conducted her orchestra. Voices soared from the choir room where joyful noises to the Lord were often snatched in two by Patsy's sharp criticisms. She wasn't normally so cross with her singers, but she was pregnant again after having two sets of twins: Levi and Andrew, followed within eighteen months by Peggy and Pearl. Patsy was exhausted but her husband Le'Vander glowed. Crossbows twanged under Larry's leadership and Spears flew under Samir's guidance. Rifles were sounding from across the compound along with the shouted commands of Le'Vander.

Gwen, Warrior of Atticus, wife of Atticus, heart of Atticus, surveyed her troops.

The first "graduating class" of the Refuge had been deployed to their homeworlds at Christmas this past year. One thousand soldiers, most of them having received a minimum of four year's training, had been sent home, as promised, to hold back the dark. Elders were combing the worlds in search of replacements. The children come here through portals in groups of twenty-five or less. By July, one month from now, they should have gathered one thousand new students who will train and be educated here at the Refuge for the next five to eight years -- depending on the child's proficiency. All children are accepted to the Refuge, as long as they meet Atticus' boundaries: old enough to care for themselves, but not old enough to menstruate or shave. And of course, they must proclaim their service to the Light.

Gwen took a deep breath and eyed potential graduates for this upcoming Winter's Dance. Behind her, her daughter Natalie turned one-handed cartwheels with varying degrees of success. Her left arm was in a cast and bound to her chest, a result of being too cocky. Hopefully, it was a painful enough lesson that Gwen's Little Warrior would remember.

Next to Natalie, using a practice dowel and flowing through the steps of Morning Meadow as if she were born to dance, was Natalie's younger sister, Easter. At six, she was two years younger than Natalie and looked like a miniature Atticus – blonde and solid. Their three year old sister River and six month old brother Rutger were in the nursery.

Suddenly, everyone paused. Some did so because they felt the portal opening; others only because their sparring partners had stilled. Atticus pressed his left hand over his throbbing scar. Ben and Pierre were going to visit Otka and see to her sick dragons. As suddenly as the sensation started, it stopped.

"Good job! Those of you who felt the portal opening, good job," Atticus heard his wife praise the young soldiers.

All soldiers were trained in two areas – physical and metaphysical. Whichever was their strongest was used defensively. The other was used offensively; the thought being that they were coming to 'hold back the dark', not destroy it. They went to save and rescue innocents, not conquer the already fallen.

Atticus sighed with relief as the pain disappeared and got back to the endless pile of paperwork, his sermon on the Tower of Babel forgotten.

4 JOHN PARKER

John Parker took his pack off and popped his neck – first one side, then the other. He rolled his shoulders and leaned against the white railings that bordered the Ranch. He felt the portal open and close – that's what made him notice the ranch. He watched the horses being worked through obstacle courses in the lush green fields. Small creatures called dogs worked beside the horses and people rode the horses or ran beside them.

John stared at each one, trying to see a familiar face. "Where are you, girly girl?" he whispered.

John stood there, leaning on the fence, for over an hour. He would have stayed there all day, except a white van pulled up beside him and a man called out, "Hey, I am going into town. Do you want a ride?"

John had spent most of his life taking advantage of happenstance. "Thanks, mister." As he climbed into the passenger side of the van, he held out his hand, "I'm John Parker."

The driver shook his hand, "I am Samir Ahmadinaja."

John used the gosh-golly grin that worked well with strangers, "You're not from around here, originally, are you?"

"Oh," Samir laughed. "Who is?"

John Parker, who used to be called Stelt, laughed.

5 A SWIFT KISS

Wren-at-Dawn was a man of his word. He repeated the same phrase to himself as he got up early Sunday morning to live up to his lost bet. He'd do all the stables today – his first day in charge while Pierre was off-world with Ben. But he would take two hours off for church. He would go to church because Atticus was a wise minister and the music lifted his spirits. It had nothing to do with the new recruit named Lanza who sang in the choir. Well, not much.

Lost in thoughts of a sweet face, silver-white hair and the voice of an angel, Wren-at-Dawn jumped when Hreno said, "See, I told you he'd be here by now."

Jeremy, accompanied by his best friend Magyar, nodded and picked up a pitchfork.

"I'm going to lay down over here, Jeremy," the dog said. The boy nodded.

Jeremy and Magyar spent their summers at the Ranch. Five years earlier, Jeremy had been one of the students kidnapped by a Strategia Oscuro during the Battle of Crystal Lake. Magyar had risked her life to rescue him. Hreno and Wren-at-Dawn had been part of the portal which brought him home. He had to repeat the seventh grade that year, but from that point on, he knew what he wanted out of life – to be a veterinarian – and he did everything it took to reach that goal. His tests and grades were good enough to go to one of the International Baccalaureates or Collegiate High Schools in the county, but George Jenkins High had one of the best agricultural departments, so he refused their invitations. He was a junior there now with a 3. 9 GPA. He'd been given a full four-year scholarship to UF and would work on his veterinarian degree along with his bachelors. The scholarship was from the Refuge. He was proud of that. And he knew that as soon as he was able, he'd move up here and become Ben's partner. Ben was the best vet anywhere, all the animals agreed on that. But they also felt it wouldn't hurt to have one who could talk to animals, like Jeremy could.

"I still can't believe the Queen didn't get her way." Hreno brought an empty wheelbarrow over to Wren-at-Dawn.

"It's about time Ben stood up to her. She's become a spoiled brat." He took off his shirt. With his exertion, the normally pale scar bisecting the area between his left shoulder and collarbone was a vivid red against his tanned skin. He rarely noticed the scar anymore, except when an extremely powerful portal was being woven. Then it ached and burned.

Jeremy took off his shirt, too. It wasn't that he was mimicking his hero; it was just warm in the stable. "More like spoiled pet. That's what the horses call her."

"A pet? That's how they feel about her?" Hreno sneezed.

Jeremy nodded before sneezing, too.

"Bless you," Wren-at-Dawn said. "What she needs is a swift kick."

Jeremy sneezed again. "Really?" He stopped what he was doing to stare at his hero. Wren-at-Dawn was probably only a year or two older than Jeremy, but where Jeremy was still a high school kid, Wren-at-Dawn was a man. And Wren-at-Dawn thought that what Venutha needed was a swift kiss. He could do that. He could kiss the Queen.

With Hreno's and Jeremy's help, Wren-at-Dawn only had one stable left to do. They were showered and dressed for church and whistling up horses when Magyar rubbed her head against

Jeremy's leg. He bent down and cupped her head lovingly in his hands.

"I'm going to stay in the bunkhouse while you go on to church."

"Are you OK?" Jeremy asked.

"Sure. It's just been a long morning. And Ohamaha has started nesting, so I'd just as soon stay out of her way for a while."

The boy pressed soft kisses on his dog's forehead. "I love you."

"I love you, too."

Hreno put her hand on his elbow as they watched the ancient warrior pad slowly back to the boy's bunkhouse. Jeremy looked down at her, tears filling his eyes, "She's dying."

Hreno nodded but didn't say anything. She was great that way.

Chinan pulled the truck up to the farmhouse. The truck's front right headlight was busted.

"What happened?" Wren-at-Dawn asked calmly.

Chinan shook his head and tried to match the horseman's reserve. "I went into town this morning."

The truck bounced as a dozen teens climbed into the truck bed or the backseat – depending on their seniority.

"Courtney's a pretty girl," Wren-at-Dawn nodded.

"I met with her family at Bob Evans. They're good people. And they like me."

"Crazy people," Jeremy gently shoved the young horseman's head toward the steering wheel.

"When I came out, the light was busted." He picked a wadded piece of paper up and handed it to Wren-at-Dawn. "This was on the windshield. I can't read, but it made Courtney blush and her father got angry and said perhaps I should think about moving into town."

Wren-at-Dawn handed the paper to Jeremy. "And?"

13

"And start going to First Baptist."

Jeremy read the message aloud, "Go home you damned freaks."

"You shouldn't have gone alone."

Jeremy scowled but didn't question Wren-at-Dawn in front of the others.

"Take a dog with you, or let one of the other horsemen ride along."

"Yes, Wren-at-Dawn."

"Make sure all the Horsemen and Dog Guards know this. There are some people in town who have their minds set to hate us. We don't need any trouble while Pop and Dad are away."

Hreno leaned into Jeremy's ear and whispered, "Atticus and the priest of First Baptist are having talks. But not a week goes by that one of our trucks doesn't get damaged – slashed tires, busted lights, dented panels. And they like leaving nasty messages on the windshield or painted on the doors."

Venusha leaned into him from the other side, "Sometimes they pee in the cab. We have to lock the doors."

6 THE ONE WHO GUARDS THE DOOR

Five thousand people filled the sanctuary. Most of them were children, but at least a thousand of them were adults from the surrounding countryside. Morning Creek the town had doubled in population in eight short years. About one hundred of the attendees were not church members. But everyone entering the compound was secretly photographed and catalogued in Taralyn's database and cross-checked with Morgan through the IIA. Atticus glanced at his wife. Eight years ago, he'd boasted to her that he had "nigh on twenty-four members" of his church. Beside Gwen, their daughter Natalie waved at him and then turned back to her signed conversation with Chi's son, Kayien.

Across the sanctuary, a woman in her late forties sat beside Becky and Gabriel Iglesias. She must be Debbie Leedy, the sheriff's widowed mother-in-law. Debbie looked around her at the congregation. She had an air of exhaustion about her, but steeliness, too. Atticus would need to meet with her soon.

A slight commotion stirred through the children as Wren-at-Dawn and his horsemen along with Venutha and her dog guards entered the sanctuary. Dogs of every size and breed dashed up and down the aisles, greeting special friends. With a solemnity that only added to the mystique surrounding the Horsemen and Dog Guards of Atticus, Wren-at-Dawn led his three dozen humans to their pews and sat down. Venutha whistled once and the dogs settled around the sanctuary beside friends and strangers alike. It looked random, but Jeremy had admitted to Atticus that the dogs stationed themselves strategically around the church, always on guard and ready to defend the Refuge against the darkness.

Atticus cocked his head and listened to the introit. It was haunting and joyful at the same time. A short-haired mix of lab and shepherd wandered up the central aisle, sniffing the air. He stopped beside Gabriel and then pressed his way through the pew until he came to Debbie. The widow looked unsure. The dog put his head on her knee and wagged his tail. She pressed both hands on top of his head and smiled. Her grandchildren quickly scooted down and patted the vacated pew cushion. The dog jumped up and lay down with his head in Debbie's lap.

The introit ended and Beatrice Horne stood to lead the congregation through the call to worship and the prayer of confession. Bea had transformed over the last eight years, too. Almost thirty years ago, her son had died in a tragic accident which took the lives of the high school's entire football team. Her husband drank himself to death not too many years later. Now she was the den mother of one of the dormitories and called *Mother Bea* by over one thousand children. At seventy, her hair was curly grey and her plump figure made her seem to be a grandmotherly character straight off the canvas of a Norman Rockwell painting.

She had healed, but she still put fresh flowers on her son's grave every week.

Atticus felt power slowly building and looked at its source. Mitchell, sitting with his dorm of prayer warriors, was glowing. His eyes were focused inward and he seemed oblivious to his environment. Beside him, the blind girl he had rescued during the Battle of Crystal Lake leaned toward him and whispered something. The glowing stopped as Mitchell blinked. She took his hand and patted it. With the light streaming through the stained glass, it was hard to notice her olive skin was mottled with white scars from a fire which had ravaged her body and stolen her eyes. She called herself Shadow.

Avery, Morgan's son-in-law stood and walked to the Presbytery. Both of Morgan's daughters and their families moved to Morning Creek the year after their mother died. She died the same day as Rutger Perkins, the same day as the Battle of Crystal Lake. Shane and Missy lived next door to Gabriel. Suz and Avery lived two blocks away. Avery cleared his throat and addressed the congregation. "The word for today comes from the Gospel of John of Jesus the Bringer of Light. Chapter ten verse three. *The one who guards the door opens it for him. And the sheep listen to the voice of the shepherd. He calls his own sheep by name and leads them out.*"

On a screen, the same verse was projected in English and other languages. It continued rolling through the various languages as the choir stood. A beautiful girl with white hair and icy blue eyes stood with the choir and then stepped forward to the soloist mike. Had she been from Earth, her face would have been described as oriental-looking. A slight rustling came from the horsemen and dog guards as Wren-at-Dawn leaned forward, perching on the edge of his pew. His friends rolled their eyes and grinned at each other, but the young man only saw the singer.

The choir sang the verses in eight-part harmony, but the young girl sang the refrain by herself, "Some through the waters, some through the flood, some through the fire, but all through the blood. Some through great sorrow but God gives a song, In the night season and all the day long."

Patsy was right; Lanza was powerful. Atticus took note of the people who hung their heads and sobbed; the elders would visit with each one this week – to heal, to console, to minister to.

As the choir sat, Atticus arose. Le'Vander nodded at him from the sound booth, letting him know his walk-around mike was live. He hadn't needed a mike in the old church when he only had two dozen parishioners. Atticus pushed the childish thought away.

"Through," he stated. "Through. The choir just sang to us about God leading us through. Not to. Not from. But through."

He stepped thoughtfully down the altar steps, pausing on each one. "God leads us through many situations. He leads me through the valley of the shadow of death. He leads me through the flood. He leads me through the fire. God leads me through the Portals of Light. God even leads some people through the Doors of Despair."

Atticus nodded. "Through. You know where else God leads me? He leads me beside. Beside the still waters. He leads me along the paths of righteousness. And what about those wonderful green pastures? Our horsemen know about the importance of green pastures!"

Atticus pointed, "Wren-at-Dawn, what happens if horses stay too long in a green pasture?"

The young man reddened, glanced in Lanza's direction, and stood. "All of the grass gets eaten or stomped down and the horses starve."

Atticus nodded. Wren-at-Dawn grinned and sat back down.

"On this world, we have a saying, 'still waters run deep. '"

Debbie's eyebrows wrinkled in a questioning frown as she mulled over the words, 'on this world', but she continued stroking the lush fur of the dog sleeping in her lap.

"Still waters run deep," Atticus repeated. "Deep waters. Deep sorrows. Deep grief. Deep anger. Deep despair. Deep regret. Deep waters, yes? If God led us into these still waters, we would drown. So God leads us beside them, until we have gone past them."

Atticus walked back up the steps. "Fire. All of you know what fire does to flesh. Some of you know personally what it feels like to be burned. Hold your hand in the flame and the flesh boils, blisters, melts, and burns. But if you move quickly enough through the flames... Will it singe you? Yes. Will it burn you?

Maybe. Will it ignite your clothing and other things you carry with you? It could. But will it consume you? No. Sometimes, the only path to safety lies *through* the fire."

Mitchell leaned over and kissed Shadow's forehead.

"Through." Atticus stood at his pulpit. "We're not here to stay. None of us will spend eternity in this safe Refuge. The comfortable beds, the wonderful food, the loving friends and family; these are green pastures God is letting us rest in. Not stay in, just rest, for a time. The fires, the floods, the darkness and despair, these are just the still waters God is walking us beside. We're on a journey. We're on a journey home, where we will dwell in the House of the Lord forever!"

Shouts of 'amen' and 'Selah' rippled through the assembly.

"John ten, three, the guardian opens the portal for you, and God calls you. You hear God's voice and answer him and GOD WILL LEAD YOU THROUGH."

Atticus paced. "God led you here. Some through the waters, some through the flood. Some through the fire, but all through the blood. But this is not your final destination. Listen. God's calling your name. Listen. The portal is being opened for you and God is calling your name. When you answer Him and He leads you through, don't expect it to be all green pastures. Don't expect it to be all fire and flood either. But know, that when God calls you and leads you through, He will surely lead you home.

"And what does He promise us about heaven? No more what?"

"Sorrow!" someone shouted.

"No more tears!"

"No more flood!"

"No more dark soldiers!"

Everyone laughed.

Atticus surveyed his people. "When God calls your name, allow Him to lead you through."

After church, the horsemen, dog guards, and several friends went to the Jamaican Me Hungry Hall for lunch. Lanza was with Wren-at-Dawn, sitting next to him in the place Venutha usually sat. Venutha's glare was not lost on Jeremy, who called to her, "Come sit with us."

Hreno scooted over to make room between her and Jeremy.

Venutha glared again at Wren-at-Dawn, who saw nothing other than the girl at his side.

"Well, I wonder what Pop and Dad are doing now. I bet they are surrounded by dragons."

Venutha's face clouded even more at Jeremy's words.

Jeremy continued, pulling everyone at the table into his scheme, "Yeah, I bet they're having the time of their lives. Big old dragons with wing spans the size of a house and claws like giant bulldozers and fire shooting left and right."

Venutha took a deep breath as Gamga barked words of temperance to her from his place at Joan's side. "I'm sure they are," she said primly.

Jeremy was not to be dissuaded. "I wonder if they're getting to fly on the dragons. Hey, Hreno," Jeremy leaned with exaggeration around the front of Venutha. "Do you think they're getting to fly on the dragons?"

Gamga growled again, but Venutha whined, "It's not fair!" People around her laughed.

"I could talk to dragons. I know I could. I could have helped Dad. I should have gotten to go!"

Jeremy turned to face her, aware that every eye in the mess hall was on him. "You know what you need, Queen Venutha?"

She knew she had a nickname, but no one said it to her face, so she opened her eyes and mouth in surprise.

That's when Jeremy made his move. His hands grabbed her shoulders, his lips made contact with hers, and he gave her exactly what Wren-at-Dawn had suggested – a swift kiss.

She decked him, knocking him backwards off the bench.

From his less than noble place sprawling on the floor, Jeremy shouted, "What did you do that for?"

"You kissed me!" She stood over him.

"Yeah, well," he sat up. "It's what you deserved."

"What?" She placed her hands on her hips as Wren-at-Dawn helped Jeremy to his feet. "I'm not your girlfriend!"

"Yeah, well, I wasn't kissing you like you were my girlfriend."

Wren-at-Dawn asked, "Why were you kissing her?"

"You told me to!" Jeremy shouted. "You said the Queen was being a whiny brat and what she needed was a swift kiss!"

Venutha bellowed, "You told him to kiss me?"

Wren-at-Dawn lowered his voice and spoke slowly. "A swift kick. Kick, not kiss."

"Oh." Jeremy tried not to look at everyone staring at him.

With an icy edge to her soft voice, Venutha hissed, "You told him to kick me?"

Hreno took Venutha's right arm and Lanza took her left. They walked with her outside, leaving Wren-at-Dawn and Jeremy without a backward glance.

"She hit me." Jeremy sat on his cot and stroked Magyar's back. "I kissed her; she hit me. Everyone thinks I'm an idiot."

His dog huffed gently in that way dogs laugh.

"I brought you a treat. Chicken meat, just the way you like it."

"Thanks, boy. Why don't you put it under the pillow. I'll eat it later. Not very hungry right now."

"Are you cold?" Jeremy drew a blanket over her.

She sighed. "Just lay here beside me for a while, won't you?"

He stretched out, curling around her and pressing his cheek into the soft fur behind her ears.

21

"Jeremy, you know I love you. From the moment I saw you, I knew you were my boy and I was your girl."

"Yes. From the very first moment, when you rescued me from Marcelux."

"You're going to be a wonderful vet."

"I hope so."

"I know so." She drew a deep breath. "Don't forget me, Jeremy."

He began to cry. "I won't. Not ever."

"But don't let the memory of me block out being able to love someone else."

"I won't, Magyar."

"I love you, boy."

"Love you. I love you."

She took another deep, shuddering breath and then passed away.

The boy held her, sobbing.

He felt Gamga at his side. The old police dog nosed his arm and pressed against Magyar's body. Then he tilted his head back and howled.

7 FOR THE LOVE OF MAGYAR

Debbie sat under the shade of a Norfolk pine on the marble slab of someone named Rutger "Perkins" Pardulfo. She didn't want to intrude on the funeral; she was supposed to be at the mall. When Gabriel got the phone call Sunday evening that a friend of his had died, he sobbed. Debbie had never seen Gabriel cry, and she'd known him since he was a boy.

Debbie was supposed to drop the family at the church and then go on, but she watched them walk into a crowd of hundreds of people who all hugged and kissed each other and got curious about this Magyar. She walked behind the procession to a field of poppies and then wandered through the field until she came to where she was now. She could see a massive crowd. She could barely hear the eulogy, just sounds, not words. It was peaceful here, with the breeze swirling the red and pink blossoms.

A woman in her late sixties stood off to the side, watching the funeral. Debbie watched as the woman put down her basket of wildflowers and covered her face. Her shoulders shook as she wept.

Debbie looked down and away, anywhere but at the older woman, crying alone. Ashamed of her own cowardice, Debbie stood and walked over to her.

Softly, so as not to startle her, Debbie said, "Blessed are those who mourn, for they shall be comforted."

Bea looked up and wiped her eyes.

"Here," Debbie handed her a kerchief. "My foster mother told me to always keep a clean hanky in my pocket. Just in case."

The woman laughed and used the hanky to wipe her eyes. "And clean underwear, in case you get in an accident."

"Lord, yes," Debbie smiled. "Was she a friend of yours?"

"Magyar? Yes. I suppose she was. She was a dog, you know."

"A dog? They're holding a funeral for a dog?"

Bea sniffed and pocketed the hanky. "You see all those children there? About three hundred of them are my foster children. They'd be dead, or worse, if it hadn't been for that sweet dog, and others, like your son-in-law."

"I don't understand."

"The Battle of Crystal Lake. Hasn't Gabriel ever mentioned it to you?"

From across the field, a duet of Matt and Juan began to sing 'Oh Jesus Bread of Life. '

Debbie looked down at the ground, uncomfortable with lying, "No."

"Good answer. The sheriff would be proud of you. That's the correct answer to a total stranger. But I'm an elder of the Refuge. My name's Beatrice Horne, but most just call me Mother Bea. The Battle of Crystal Lake was when we knew for sure that the war had found us. That man, you were sitting on his monument; yes, I saw you. He died during that battle. He gave his life so those five thousand children could be saved. There were only a handful of our members that did what it took to save them. It nearly divided the church, the fact that they went against Atticus. But five thousand children were rescued that day.

"See that tall boy with his hands on the casket, crying like the world is coming to an end? His name is Jeremy Dart. He was one of the children stolen from Crystal Lake Middle. That dog braved soldiers of the foulest kind and personally rescued that boy. So, yes. We're having a funeral for a dog."

"My best friend Rosa had a dog when I was a little girl. When he died, I thought our hearts would break."

"Dogs have souls, you know."

Debbie looked at Bea and then as if afraid to admit it, nodded in agreement.

Dogs began to howl, singly and then en masse. The hairs along Debbie's arms raised, and she felt tears spring to her eyes.

Monday night, after the funeral, the boys and men in his bunkhouse settled down to sleep, but Jeremy just lay there. This was the first night in five years that he had slept alone.

About two in the morning, he felt a hand touch his shoulder. He wasn't asleep, but he'd had his eyes closed. Venutha knelt beside him and whispered, "Ohamaha is having her puppies. She wants you to come help. They're early. She needs your help, Jeremy. Please come."

"Are you crying?" He sat up.

"Yes," she gasped. "Oh, Jeremy. I'm so sorry about Magyar." She threw her arms around him and he clung to her, then pushed her away. "Let's go help Ohamaha."

By dawn, seven squeaky little balls of golden and black fur were attached to Ohamaha's teats. The new mother spoke softly, "Thank you, Jeremy. You helped me through the night."

He rubbed her ears, "You helped me through the night, too."

8 LINES

"Mother, you do not have to hang your clothes on the line. We have a perfectly good dryer."

Debbie snapped a skirt before pinning it to the line. "We also have a perfectly good Earth and I'd like to help keep it that way."

Becky took a deep breath. "Turning the drier on a few more times a week isn't going to cause a nuclear winter."

"I saved forty dollars a month on electricity by hanging our clothes out on the line."

Becky closed her eyes and gritted her teeth at the old story, remembering the embarrassment of a teen-ager whose mother hung their clothes out.

"Hey!" Gabriel stuck his head out the back door. "There you are. The kids are ready for Morning Meadow. You coming?"

Becky smiled at her husband. "Yes. We're coming."

Debbie bent down and picked up a wet shirt. "No, *we're* not. *You* are. I've got things to do here."

"Mom, you need to get involved with the activities around here. It'll be good for you."

Debbie snapped the cotton blouse and pinned it by the collar.

Gabriel ventured into the back yard, stepping his way carefully between the deadly silence. Wife? Or mother-in-law? Which one first?

"You know, Mom, I always loved it that you took time to hang out your clothes. They smelled so good."

The expressions on the women's faces told him everything: he'd won major points with Debbie, but would most likely be sleeping on the couch for a while.

"Hey, we're going to be late!" Thomas shouted from inside.

"We'll be back in a few hours. Don't forget, we've got the cookout tonight at Morgan's," Gabriel gently took his wife's arm.

"Grandpa Morgan's home?" Thomas shouted, "Devin, Grandpa Morgan's home!"

Debbie bent down, ignoring the people she now lived with and was dependent on.

"Give her time," she heard Gabriel whisper. "It's a lot to adjust to, even without the Refuge."

9 BORN IN A BARN

"I don't know why I couldn't go, too, that's all." Venutha was on Dusk-Wind's back, waiting her turn to practice swooping down and picking up a thirty-pound sack of dirt. It was a simulation of grabbing up a small child and remaining on horseback. "I would have served a vital role as interpreter."

"Give it a rest," Wren-at-Dawn growled.

"Otka speaks to the dragons. She doesn't need you," Jeremy added.

"Well, Dad didn't need to take Papa Pierre. What good would he do?"

Jeremy and Wren-at-Dawn glanced at each other and grinned.

"What?" Venutha snorted.

"It's your turn," Wren-at-Dawn said calmly.

She glowered and spoke to her horse. They efficiently – and gracefully – made their way through the obstacle course.

Back in the stables, with Hreno to back her up, Venutha started again. "Papa Pierre doesn't even like dragons; I heard him tell Dad that. You did, too, didn't you, Hreno?"

The girl in question squealed and ran flapping her arms in the air toward the couple getting out of a car: Mitchell and Shadow.

Jeremy clapped his hands on his horse's muzzle to calm her, "Why do girls do that? Why?"

Wren-at-Dawn rolled his eyes.

"Otka doesn't need Dad and Pierre."

Jeremy turned on her, "What? Were you born in a barn? Papa Pierre isn't there to see dragons. He isn't there to help Daddy Ben. He's there to see Otka."

Venutha stared at him with her mouth open. His words about being born in a barn were supposed to have been funny. But they weren't. They hurt.

"Come on," Wren-at-Dawn took Jeremy's arm. "She doesn't understand; she's just a child."

She watched them walk away. Hreno, arm in arm with Mitchell and Shadow, was heading to the Big House. Jeremy and Wren-at-Dawn were heading to the bath house. Ohamaha was occupied with her latest litter of adorable puppies. Joan was busy baking for tonight's cookout. "I wasn't born in a barn," Venutha said. "I was raised by horses, but I wasn't born in a barn."

"I was," Runs-at-Water's-Edge said. "So were my colts."

"And I'm not a child."

"Is that what he said?"

She nodded, fresh tears springing to her eyes.

Runs-at-Water's-Edge shook her mane. "I have never understood why the human mating ritual has to be so complex. You should be more like horses. We go into heat, we mate, we have foals. It's very simple."

"I haven't come into heat yet." Venutha wiped her eyes.

"Are you old enough?"

"I don't know." She shrugged. "I don't know how old I am. I know I've been here almost seven years. And I lived with the horses for a long time, but we didn't keep track of time. Not like humans do."

"No, not like humans."

"So I'm about sixteen years old, or maybe thirteen."

"You know what you need?" Awohah, one of Ohamaha's second litter, spoke up. "You need boobs. In the bunkhouse at night, Jeremy and the other boys talk about boobs a lot. You don't have any boobs."

"Joan doesn't have boobs," Venutha countered.

"Yes she does. How else would she nurse Baby Ben and the new baby?" Runs-at-Water's-Edge said.

"No, no, I'm not talking about nursing teats. I'm talking BOOBS. Jeremy says, 'the bigger the better.' You don't have any. Seems to me, they'd get in the way, but what do I know about human anatomy. I'm not human."

Venutha crossed her arms over her flat chest, hung her head, and walked out of the barn.

"I tell you," she heard Runs-at-Water's-Edge say. "Human mating rituals are way too complicated."

"Now, what could be so terrible to make such a beautiful young lady look so unhappy?"

Venutha glanced up from her latte at the man standing next to her table. She had gone to the bookstore in town to think.

He held up his hands, palms forward. "I know. You're not supposed to talk to strangers, but I'm not really a stranger. We go to the same church: The Refuge."

"Oh."

"There's no reason to remember me, I mean," he grinned and gestured down his thin frame. "Look at me. Nothing to write home about. That's what the Earthers say, isn't it? Course you wouldn't have noticed me."

"No, I do. I mean, I think I do."

"Look, just to let you know I'm not lying, I'll tell you your name. You're Venutha, and your best friend is Hreno. Am I right?"

Venutha nodded. "Hreno and I are adopted sisters."

"Yes, you are clan-sisters. See, I do know you." He smiled. "Oh, what am I thinking? Your coffee's getting cold. Let me buy you another one. You don't mind if I sit with you while I take a break? I work here. My name's John Parker."

10 GRANDPA MORGAN

When Atticus had a house built inside the compound four years ago, Morgan bought the parsonage. He liked the simplicity of the two-bedroom house with the barbecue pit in the backyard. He didn't get there as often as he'd like to, but whenever he arrived, he usually threw a cookout his first night back. His daughters and their families lived in Morning Creek, and all of his friends lived either in town or on the compound, so the parsonage was a good gathering spot.

He heard the horses and dogs as he lit the coals. He went to greet them. He wasn't a hugger, but he hugged these people as he welcomed them inside.

"Ben and Pierre are still with Otka's dragons." Joan kissed his cheek and went to the ever ready play pen to put Baby Ben down. Morgan watched her swollen body with an old twinge of regret. He knew he never really had a chance with her, but he cared for her.

In a quick flurry of embraces, he greeted Venutha, Wren-at-Dawn, Hreno, and Jeremy. "I was sorry to hear about Magyar, son."

The boy nodded.

Morgan went out to help Le'Vander and Patsy wrestle two sets of twins out of the car seats from inside their van. Patsy looked like she was expecting another set, but she assured Morgan this was just one – "the last one," said with a glare in Le'Vander's direction.

Missy's family came and he swooped his granddaughters through the air while being kissed and hugged. Then shouts of "Grandpa Morgan!" announced the arrival of his other daughter's family, followed immediately by their neighbors, Gabriel and Becky, their boys and Debbie.

Morgan had run her clearance through the elders when Gabriel told him she was coming to live here, so he'd seen pictures of her. But as she stepped out of the Nissan in her cotton batik skirt, cowl-necked shirt and canvas shoes, he was struck by her appearance. She had a beauty that cameras obviously could not catch. A solemnity that set her apart, aloof but not superior. He was reminded of a phrase by ee cummings he learned in college, 'i, alone and afraid, in a world i never made. '

And then she was shaking his hand and smiling graciously, thanking him for including her in tonight's festivities.

Everyone brought food to add to the burgers he had on the grill.

The children raced around with the dogs while the horses meandered through the pecan grove behind his yard.

The Sveets and Shadow came, as did Taralyn and Doug, and Tyler and Ricean. Morgan lost himself in his role of host, wishing he'd had a life filled with such opportunities, but knowing it wouldn't have been possible before his wife died.

He glanced around and found that Debbie was seated in a wicker couch he'd set up under the oak tree. She had a cloth bag by her feet and seemed to be doing something with a bright blue piece of string. As he watched, she moved her fingers and wrists so that the yarn danced around a stick with a hook at the end. The beginnings of something round took shape.

"Grandpa Morgan, watch me!" Cheyenne yelled as she cartwheeled across the yard. He applauded.

To his right, he could hear Patsy and Venutha laughing. Jeremy and Wren-at-Dawn moved closer to Venutha. Patsy sounded happy tonight, "I swear, Venutha, you look absolutely radiant. You must have met a boy."

Venutha reddened and the boys snorted in disbelief. She narrowed her eyes and then took a deep breath, "As a matter of fact, he's not a boy at all. He's a man. And unlike some children I could mention, he doesn't believe I was born in a barn."

She flounced past Jeremy and Wren-at-Dawn and went to speak with Runs-at-Water's-Edge.

Within minutes, the blue yarn had formed a small circle no bigger than Debbie's palm. She glanced up, feeling she was being watched. Hreno sat on the ground, staring at her hands intently. Debbie smiled and held the blue circle out to the pretty teen. Hreno crept closer and perched beside her.

"This is called crochet," Debbie spoke softly, because the girl looked so frightened.

"You're weaving."

"No, weaving is two dimensional using many strands within an inner-locking frame. This is one piece of yarn and one hook and I make three dimensional pieces. See? I take the yarn, grab it with the hook, and pull it through to make stitches. The stitches form a design and I can change the yarn to make a pattern."

"What will it become?" the girl whispered.

"A cap for a baby. See how the sides are beginning to curl in? This is the crown of the cap."

"But," she reached out to touch the offered piece. "What does it do?"

"It keeps the baby's head warm. It protects the baby."

Hreno's mouth flew open. Debbie smiled. "Would you like to learn?"

She closed her lips and nodded vigorously. "I can't teach anyone to weave. I just weave. I become a portal, so that others may pass through. But it would be wonderful if I could keep them safe, too."

Morgan watched Debbie tilt her head sideways as she spoke with Hreno. He couldn't hear their words, but judging from the expressions on their faces, the conversation was eye-opening for both of them. He casually moved closer.

"I love making caps for babies. I make little booties and blankets for them, too. I also make things for children and adults: sweaters, shawls, scarves; it's fun. I think the first thing we'll make is a cap for you. To keep your head warm this winter."

"Really?"

"Yes, really. What color would you like?"

"It can be different colors?"

"Absolutely. I live with Gabriel Iglesias the sheriff. Why don't you ask your parents if you can come Monday morning and I'll teach you how to crochet?"

"I have no parents. My mother was sold soon after my birth and my father became my redeemer when he turned to despair. And then we became separated when we were imprisoned before I escaped to the Refuge."

Debbie blinked. "Oh."

"But I will ask Joan."

Morgan grabbed the arm of a boy racing past and bent down to whisper, "Go ask your grandmother if she's OK."

"Which one is Joan?"

Hreno pointed them out as she named her family. "Joan, she's pregnant, and I also live with Venutha who is speaking with Runs-at-Water's-Edge."

"The horse?"

"Yes. And Jeremy – he speaks with animals, too."

"His dog just died."

"Yes. And I also live with Wren-at-Dawn. He is a weave, like me, but he was almost redeemed before he came here, so he doesn't talk about it much. And I live with Daddy Ben and Poppa Pierre, but they've gone to take care of Otka's dragons. They're sick. And I live with all the Dog Guards and Horsemen of Atticus."

Devin pushed his way onto the couch and snuggled against his grandmother. "What you making, Grandma?"

"A cap." The bell shape was evident now.

"Grandmother Debbie is going to teach me to crochet."

"She's good at it. She made me a sweater with a dinosaur on it when I was little."

"What's a dinosaur?"

"It's like a dragon."

Hreno gasped. "Could you teach me this?"

"Yes. It may take a while, but if you want to learn, I'll show you."

"I could make a dragon sweater for Venutha. Then she won't be so mad all the time."

"The fun of crocheting is making gifts for others," Debbie smiled.

"I'll go ask Joan now," Hreno stood. "Goodbye, Grandmother Debbie."

Devin tilted his head up at her. "We've decided that everyone gets to call you Grandma Debbie, since everyone gets to call Cheyenne's grandfather Grandpa Morgan."

"That's nice. I like that idea."

"Hreno's a weave."

"So she said."

"She's been on hundreds of different worlds."

"She's a very polite young lady."

"You OK with all this, Grandma?"

Debbie grinned, not realizing Morgan was listening. "I've read every book by Ray Bradbury and Robert Heinlein and Douglas Adams and James P. Hogan. I grew up watching Star Trek and Lost in Space. Honey, I am so OK with this. I've been waiting for this all my life." She leaned over and kissed him. He hugged her neck and dashed away.

Morgan caught a hint of her cologne – Green Tea – and inhaled deeply. Debbie was OK with "this".

Patsy sank heavily beside Debbie, moaning slightly. "Lord, I shouldn't have eaten that peach cobbler, but your daughter Becky sure makes a good one."

"Thanks." Debbie held out the completed cap. "I understand you're having a boy. I made this for him. Booties and blanket to follow."

"Oh! This is just the cutest little thing!" She took it and laughed. "Thank you."

"You're welcome. Have you decided on a name?"

"Well," she moaned again and stretched, trying to get comfortable. "We were thinking of naming him Rutger, but Gwen's already got a son named after him."

"Rutger, the man who died at the Battle of Crystal Lake and has the monument over in the poppy field?"

"Yes. He walked me down the aisle when I married Le'Vander. Oh, man, that hurts."

Debbie frowned. She gently reached over and pressed her fingers against Patsy's abdomen. "Is this your first child?"

"Lord no, I've got Levi and Andrew, and then Peggy and Pearl. I told my husband if this one was twins again, he was going in for a little nip and tuck, if you know what I mean." Patsy made scissor-gestures with one hand while pressing the other to her aching side.

"Patsy, you don't know me, so please don't take offense, but I think you're in labor."

"No, no, it's too early. I've got another month at least. LORD!!!" She bellowed the last word.

Morgan shouted, "Le'Vander! Somebody get Le'Vander!"

"It's alright, Patsy. You know how to do the breathing? Ha, ha, ha, ha, ha. That's right." Debbie placed both hands on the rigid abdomen. "You're right in the middle of a contraction. Let it wash over you. Don't fight it; it's just like a wave in the ocean."

"But it hurts!" Patsy shuddered.

"Of course it hurts. Every ounce of pleasure costs a pound of pain. It'll be worth it. Once you see that baby in your arms, it'll be worth all the pain in the world."

"I'm here. I'm here, Patsy. My Patsy Cline," Le'Vander grabbed her hands.

Debbie firmly gripped his elbow. "Breathe with her. The contraction's almost over. Breath, like you've practiced."

Le'Vander led Patsy in the breathing exercise and Debbie stood. "Gabriel, crank up the sirens. Put Patsy and Le'Vander in your cruiser. Morgan, call ahead to the hospital, let them know she's on her way, and she only has about twenty minutes of labor left. The baby's already dropped. Ladies, gather up the children, keep them out of the way but let them know this is just a normal part of life. Hreno, you and yours might want to ride ahead and let your preacher know."

"But, my babies!"

"I'll take care of them, Patsy," Morgan assured her.

Debbie braced the small of her back and looped Patsy's arm over her shoulder. "The contraction's over. We're going to stand you up now and get you into Gabriel's car. He'll take you to the hospital."

"No. No, take me to the clinic. Rawan is my mid-wife." She got slowly to her feet.

"No, you're going to the hospital. Your baby's breach. You need a doctor."

"My baby's what?"

Debbie grabbed Patsy's hand. "Feel here, this is your baby's head. He hasn't turned yet. He dropped before he turned. It's alright. It happens sometimes. But you need a real doctor."

"I want Rawan!" Patsy sobbed.

Taralyn assured her as they led her out the gate and to the front yard, "She'll be there. She and Chi are both in the clinic tonight. I'm so close to delivery, I keep tabs on where they are."

"My cap! My baby's cap!" Patsy cried.

Hreno dashed up to her and pressed it into her hands.

"Chi's got a stretcher waiting by the clinic doors. And Rawan is right there." Morgan put his blackberry away.

They waved as the cruiser's lights and siren soared and it drove away.

Morgan stood beside this soft-spoken stranger who had suddenly taken charge. "I told Chi it might be breach."

Debbie nodded and glanced up at everyone still waiting for her further orders. She grinned, "Nobody touch the peach cobbler."

The tension burst in relieved laughter.

Thirty minutes later, Morgan answered his phone and shouted, proud as he could be, "It's a boy! Six pounds, nine ounces. And listen," he held the phone out. "He's already singing."

Everyone cheered. He held the phone to his ear again and his expression sombered. "Of course I will, Le'Vander. The boys can sleep in the spare room and the girls will be fine in the playpen."

The crowd stilled, trying to listen.

"Yeah, I understand." Morgan's eyes shifted to Debbie. "I'll be sure to let her know."

Debbie kissed the infant Peggy and handed her to Venutha.

"We love you both," Morgan's voice broke a little and he hung up.

Taralyn asked the question everyone had. "What's wrong?"

Morgan took a deep breath. "You know he was six weeks early. He was breach, with the chord around his neck. It took a while to revive him."

"Revive?"

"Oh my Lord."

Morgan continued, "And since he's a preemie, his crown hasn't met properly. The cap was the perfect size and fit."

Debbie lowered her eyes.

"Chi said it was exactly what will keep his head warm and protected until it grows fully."

Hreno slipped her hand into Wren-at-Dawn's. Most of the women present placed a protective hand over their abdomens.

Uncomfortable at their attention, Debbie tried to sidestep, "What's his name?"

Morgan grinned. "They can't decide between Atticus or Morgan, but his middle name is Rutger."

Debbie turned, "I'd better get started on Atticus Morgan Rutger's booties."

Morgan smiled, with just a twist of suspicion in his lips.

Debbie returned to the wicker couch and retrieved her bag. As she launched the yarn on her hook, Ricean sat beside her. She didn't speak, but she watched every move Debbie's hands and fingers made. Twenty minutes later, Debbie handed the silent Sword of Atticus a completed bootie and began the mate. Most of the pregnant women had gathered their chairs around Debbie. She noted that this circle of women were all expectant mothers except Sara, the two girls from the Ranch, Ricean and her own daughter.

As she crocheted, she wondered if there might be something which linked them, something other than the obvious – being members of the same cult. She wondered if membership was enough of a link, but her daughter wasn't pregnant.

She will be soon. The thought came unbidden and foreign into her mind. Debbie glanced at Becky in concern. She had had a difficult pregnancy and delivery with Thomas. After Devin was born by cesarean, she was warned not to get pregnant again. She never discussed her and Gabriel's solution to that problem. Becky was engulfed in Gabriel's arms, her back to his chest, as they listened to Larry and Doug boast about some adventure they'd shared.

"I can't wait to go back through a portal," Gabriel remarked. "It was incredible – to know you're standing on a different world, under a different sun and stars."

"I want to go," Becky added.

"As soon as you've mastered your weapon, I'll ask Atticus," Doug promised.

Debbie glanced at the women around her. Ricean was the only one not pregnant. The woman was about Debbie's age, just at the outer edge of her child-bearing years.

"Monday morning," Debbie spoke softly. "I am going to teach Hreno to crochet. I can as easily teach a dozen as I can one, if you'd like to come."

"What time?"

"What do I need?"

"Will there be enough room?"

Morgan's voice was a tenor harmony to the soprano and alto questions. "Why don't you use the old fellowship hall across the road? That way, you could bring your children and let them play while Debbie teaches you."

"The key's hidden behind the marble angle."

"And it's air conditioned."

"I haven't been inside since the Battle of Seyrock last autumn. It may be a bit dusty."

"When?" Taralyn repeated.

"After Morning Meadow and breakfast," Ricean said decisively.

"And what time would that be in my world?" Debbie asked coolly.

The women gaped, unsure of the tone of her words. Taralyn laughed, taking it for dry wit. "Ten o'clock. We'll meet at ten o'clock."

Debbie nodded. "You'll need one skein of 4-ply acrylic yarn in a light color and size J and M hooks. I'll teach you how to make child and adult sized caps first. And we'll go from there."

"You must make one to give away for everyone you make for yourself," Hreno had joined them. "That's what my great aunt used to say, when she wove nets for the villagers."

"I used to belong to a Prayer Shawl group. We did that, too." Debbie handed a matching bootie to Ricean, who kissed it and laughed.

"Prayer Shawl? Like a Prayer Warrior?" Joan asked.

Debbie tried to ignore Morgan's attention. "I'm not sure. In my world – yes."

"We are in your world," Joan insisted.

Debbie smiled faintly, but kept her opinion to herself.

11 CONNECTIONS

Church the next morning was a joyous event. Matt stood in for Patsy as music director and Atticus announced the arrival of Patsy and Le'Vander's boy.

"What are you doing?" Jeremy hissed at Venutha.

"What? Nothing." She sat back on the pew.

"You look like you're looking for someone."

"I might be."

"Who are you looking for?"

"A friend."

"Well, sit still and she'll find you. What, did you bathe in perfume this morning?" Jeremy rubbed his nose.

"It's not a her. It's a him. And he happens to like my cologne."

"Shush!" Wren-at-Dawn commanded. He turned his attention back to the choir and the way Lanza's lips moved as she sang.

Venutha stuck her tongue out at him. Jeremy grinned.

Debbie sat with her eyes closed. Her head ached with the remnant of a nightmare and her left shoulder twinged. She must have slept on it wrong. In her lap and sprawled beside her was the dog Venutha told her last night was named Awohah. The dog sighed deeply and Debbie rubbed his ears.

"No kidding? My kid has been begging me to take her to Gatlinburg." John Parker frothed two lattes for the couple at the counter. "I don't suppose you'd do me a favor?"

"What?" the older man asked cautiously.

"If I give you a postcard, would you mail it from Gatlinburg? Then she could – you know – have a piece of it."

"That's sweet," the woman said.

"Here," John snatched one out of his apron. "I already had it made out and stamped."

The older man hesitated but the woman took it. "Elizabeth Court. What a lovely name."

"Ah, she's a real killer, she is. I don't get to see her often; I move around a lot. So she keeps tabs on me by the postmarks. Puts pins in this huge wall map, following me around the country."

"Isn't that sweet," she smiled.

The man held out a ten.

"No, no. The latte's on me. One favor for another."

"Well, thanks," he softened.

John Parker smiled. He'd always been able to tell so much of the truth that what little – but vital – bit of it that was the lie was overlooked by all but the most cynical of listeners.

Isabel Cortez made him send out a postcard every Monday, to keep track of his whereabouts in his search for his daughter. Now that he'd found Hreno, he had to find a way to snap the leash that Earther held on him.

When he first escaped five and a half years ago – he broke the neck of an orderly at the prison's clinic, stole his clothes and identification, and left at the end of his shift – he discovered the wonder of this new planet Earth. Cars – Stelt like cars – and dancing. Stelt loved to dance. The food was tolerable, once he got the hang of money; and got some money. But he liked popcorn, the kind with butter and salt that left his hands all greasy. What he didn't like were the whores. Women and men would befriend him and take care of him, but then they wanted sex but refused to be married. That made them whores, and he killed every single one of them as punishment for their promiscuity. When he was arrested, after wandering in search of his daughter for seventeen months, he freely admitted to three of the slayings. Had they asked him about all the others, he would have admitted to them, too, but they didn't ask. While awaiting trial, she showed up – Isabel Cortez. When they were alone, she proclaimed herself as his new lord, his Strategia Oscura. She offered him freedom of a sort, if he could find his daughter.

"Of course I can find my daughter. We're connected. She's woven from me. Set me free and I'll lead you to her if she's still on this world."

It was completely the truth. Everything except, "I'll lead you to her." He would never allow Cortez near his little girl. She made his last Strategia Oscuro look meek.

He heard the bells on First Baptist's tower and took off his apron. He had the afternoon off. And he did have plans.

When Debbie arrived at the old church at 9:45 Monday morning, Morgan was waiting for her.

"I turned on the air, and started a pot of coffee. I set up the chairs in a circle. Didn't know if you'd need the tables or not." He opened the door and took the canvas satchel from her. He frowned at the weight of the bag.

"Books," she supplied. "Crochet books."

"I'll put them on the counter."

She watched him as he walked away from her toward the kitchen. He was trimly dressed in khaki jean shorts and a flowered Jimmy Buffett shirt. Leather – hand-tooled by the look of them – sandals allowed his feet a quiet passage along the Formica floor. Debbie glanced up at the florescent lights and ceiling fans. "This is nice. Thank you, Colonel."

"Actually," he brought her a mug of coffee. "It's General, or it will be soon."

"Congratulations."

He shrugged. "It means I'll only have five years before I have to retire, but I'm ready."

"A lot can happen in five years."

"A lot has."

"The first year it sleeps, the second year it creeps, the third year it leaps."

"Excuse me?"

Debbie looked down. "It's an old gardener's saying about transplants. It seems to apply to major life changes, too."

"You're very wise. It like that." He stepped closer. "I like you."

He put his arms around her and drew her into his embrace. She succumbed eagerly to his kisses.

"Grandma, wake-up."

Debbie bolted upright, muffling a little shriek.

"Geeze, sorry!" Thomas backed away.

Debbie looked at the clock beside the bed. "These damn nightmares."

"Mommy, Grandma said 'damn'!" the boy ran down the hall.

12 GRANDMOTHER SPIDER

Like in her dream, Morgan had set up the fellowship hall for her group, but unlike her dream, he did not present himself.

"He's been called away," Joan stated.

They sat in a circle: Debbie, Hreno, Joan, Ricean, and Taralyn from the cookout, as well as Bea who brought knitting needles in her bag, Gwen, and Visolela. Children from infancy through age eight played quietly on kindermats and quilts their mothers had brought.

"Since we're in a circle, the best way to learn this is to watch each other on your left and right. If you're across from me, you'll only see the back of the stitches, so help each other.

"The first step is the most individualized of all the stitches. It's called launching the yarn. No one does it the same way. The goal is to get one loop of yarn to stay on your hook but loose enough to be moved. So a slip knot works." Debbie illustrated these, "or a knitted loop. This is how I do it, but I have no idea how to teach this." She twisted the yarn on her hook and then pulled through another loop. "But it works."

She taught them how to make a basic chain, and then a single crochet through both loops and through the front loop and through the back loop.

"You now know how to make a cap," she announced to the confused women before her. "Gently pull out the yarn – all the way – and we'll start your caps."

47

She taught them the steps and gently corrected and encouraged as needed. "Chain five. Connect them in a circle. Chain two. Every time you end a row, you're going to do a slip stitch and two chains. Make five single crochets inside the circle. Now, slip stitch means you slide the hook behind the chain-two below and grab a loop and pull it through everything on your hook. Now chain two. For the first row, put two single crochet stitches through both loops in every stitch all the way around. Now, slip stitch behind the chain-two below and grab a loop and pull it through everything on your hook. Now chain two. The second row, put one single crochet through both loops of the first stitch and then two single crochets through the next stitch and repeat that all the way around. One, two. One, two. Slip stitch and chain two. Wait for everyone to catch up before we go on to the next row."

The next row was one single crochet twice and then two single crochets once all the way around. The next row just added another single crochet to the pattern: one single crochet three times and then two single crochets. Then one single crochet four times and two single crochets. Then one single crochet five times and two single crochets.

"The last row of the crown is one single crochet in both loops of each stitch all the way around. Now your crown is complete. The rest of the cap is a single crochet in each stitch, but done in the back loops. End each row with a slip stitch and chain two. When your cap is twenty-one rows down from the first back loop row, it's long enough. For the last row, turn and single crochet through both loops all around, slip stitch and tie off."

She observed them until they began to relax and had all started on the back loop rows.

"There is a rhythm to crochet. I like to repeat things while I crochet," Debbie spoke softly. "Ya'll ready? Just listen and don't rush yourself. This is my rhythm, but it will help your fingers crochet without your brain over-correcting you." She began to sing in a whispery contralto. "Many and great, O God, are Thy things, Maker of earth and sky; Thy hands have set the heavens with stars; Thy fingers spread the mountains and plains. Lo, at Thy Word the waters were formed; Deep seas obey Thy voice.

"Grant unto us communion with Thee, Thou star abiding One; Come unto us and dwell with us; With Thee are found the gifts of life, Bless us with life that has no end, Eternal life with Thee."

"That's very pretty," Gwen glanced up from her work. "Haunting, almost."

Debbie hadn't shared that song with anyone in years. Her own daughters had heard it so often growing up, they took it for granted and never asked its origin. She was fairly certain they'd never heard it elsewhere but from her; she'd never heard it sung by anyone else since she was a child. But she always heard it in her mind as she crocheted, especially when she worked on a shawl. Yes, it was haunting. Debbie sighed and pressed her lips together.

In the space of Debbie's silence, Taralyn commented, "You could do the Lord's Prayer. It has a beautiful rhythm."

"Or the Apostle's Creed," agreed Bea.

"Tyler has taught me a beautiful song, *Amazing Grace*," Ricean smiled.

"Oh, I like that one." Hreno exclaimed. Two beautiful caps lay beside her feet. "Let's do that one."

The women sang the familiar hymn together. Debbie wasn't sure, perhaps it was the result of the florescent lights and the ceiling fans, but the circle seemed to glow brighter than the rest of the fellowship hall.

"You can repeat scriptures, like the Twenty-third Psalm or Corinthians Thirteen. I have different ones for different pieces of clothing. For example, Jeremiah 29:11 is good if you're making something for a woman or man going through chaos and confusion. I say it as I stitch a whole row. "

Gwen nodded and led the women as they stitched, "For I know the plans I have for you, says the Lord. Plans to prosper you and not to harm you. Plans to give you hope and a future."

Bea glanced up from her baby blanket. "Sons are a heritage from the Lord, children a reward from Him. Like arrows in the hands of a warrior are sons born in one's youth. Blessed is the man whose quiver is full of them. They will not be put to shame when they contend with their enemies in the gate. Psalm 127:3-5."

"A little war-like, but I suppose it fits your world," Debbie grinned. "As you knit or crochet the next row, say a verse to yourself, following your own rhythm."

The lights hummed and Debbie was sure of it this time – the circle of women glowed.

Hreno patted her sandals in delight, "This empowers the stitches, like a song or a prayer warrior. This imbues the clothing with God's protection!"

"Well," Debbie hesitated, glancing around the circle. "I've always believed so."

Debbie was surprised – no one scoffed or smirked. Most actually nodded in agreement.

Each woman offered a scripture or song and the time flew.

In an hour, each one there had made a cap and most had started another one. The M hooks made adult-sized caps, the J made child-sized ones.

The bells from First Baptist's speakers rang out noon and Debbie put her yarn back inside her bag. "Keep one cap for yourself, and give the others away to your children or husband or friends."

Ricean stood and bowed, "It would be very nice to have booties to go with these caps."

"Booties are much more difficult, but I think most of you are ready to make afghans. Baby blankets. Would you like to meet again?"

Their enthusiastic agreement pleased Debbie.

"Is Thursday too soon?"

"I can't come Thursday morning. I'll be weaving–"

Gwen held a hand up, instantly silencing Hreno. She lowered her hand and spoke softly, "We have a church function Thursday morning. But Mondays seem to work well for us. Shall we set aside Monday mornings from ten to noon?"

They all agreed.

"Well, let's go to lunch at the Refuge hall and give away our caps," Gwen suggested.

The women joined hands and Bea prayed, "Sweet Lord Jesus, crochet us together like these pieces of yarn, to be used to Your glory and honor. And bless Debbie and encourage her to pray with Atticus soon, so she'll be one of us."

"Can I give you a ride to the Refuge?" Taralyn asked.

"No, thanks. I rode my bike. I'll meet you there." Debbie fought the panic that had surged in her with Bea's last sentence. These were nice women, but Debbie was certain that if praying with their leader made her *one of them*, she'd never do that. Cults. Images of dead bodies at the Jim Jones compound. Hive mentality of the Borg. She'd read too much and watched too many episodes of the Twilight Zone not to feel adamant about not praying with Atticus.

Hreno threw her arms around Debbie and kissed both cheeks. "Thank you, Grandmother Spider."

"Grandmother Spider?" Visolela repeated.

"Like in Morning Meadow?" Ricean asked.

"Yes. She doesn't weave a web, she crochets. She has only one hook. I believe she crochets." Hreno helped Gwen with her youngest baby.

"I'm not familiar with that story," Debbie lied.

"Ask your grandsons. They both know it. Your youngest does the Morning Meadow beautifully, but I believe your older boy might choose a different weapon. I was considering asking him to work with my knives this summer."

"You think Thomas would become a sword?" Taralyn sounded impressed.

"In time. He has the musculature for swords."

Debbie gritted her teeth, but after years of schooling her features so her foster mother, and then her husband wouldn't read her emotions, she knew she passed for calm if quiet. "Thank you, I'll do that."

Debbie unplugged the coffee pot and cleaned it, then turned off the AC and the lights. She walked into the dusky quiet of the little church where the Refuge had begun. It was beautiful and full of peace. She sat on the third row and crocheted another cap, this one with a size N hook, making it much larger than the ones she made earlier.

She walked her bike over to Morgan's house. She took out a brown paper sack and a pen. Quickly, as if afraid of her own actions, she scrawled, "Congratulations, General, and thanks for your help with the new Prayer Shawl group, Debbie."

She folded the large cap and shoved it in the bag and then left the bag on the rocking chair by the front door.

"So," Stelt brought Venutha a cup of coffee and straddled the chair next to her, "How's my pretty one?"

Venutha blushed. "I didn't see you yesterday at church."

"I had to work."

"Oh."

"So, you were looking for me?"

Venutha blushed a deeper red. "I wanted to introduce you to my friends."

"Friends, like Hreno?"

"And Jeremy and Wren-at-Dawn."

"Jeremy and Wren-at-Dawn. Are those boys?" His face clouded.

"Yes. They're my littermates. Well, that's what Ohamaha calls them. Like brothers."

"Not lovers?"

"No!" Her face blanched white in shock. "Gross, no!"

Stelt smiled. "That's my good girl. Is Hreno a good girl like you? Or does she have a lover?"

"Hreno's a good girl. She's sweet. She's our littermate, too."

Stelt splayed his fingers on the cold table between them, letting his sudden fury dissipate. "Good. My good girls."

Debbie sighed and snuggled closer to Morgan. They lay on a queen-sized bed with lush cotton linens and a feather down comforter. White mosquito netting swayed gently around them, separating them from the rest of the room. She smelled sun-freshened sheets and Morgan's Aramis cologne. He was kissing the top of her head and tracing squiggles along her bare skin.

"This is wonderful," he mumbled against her hair. "It's just what I always wanted."

She smiled and pressed her lips against the moist warmth just below his collarbone.

"When Annie had the accident, I put her on life support. She was in a comma for almost twenty years."

Debbie listened to words she knew were hard for Morgan to say.

"I took lovers. But I never loved them. I always loved my wife."

"We shouldn't use the same word for two such different verbs. My husband was an incredible lover, but he was pretty much useless outside of the bedroom."

Morgan pulled her back and peered into her face. "I wonder what it will be like when we make love."

A shadow passed by the mosquito netting. Something large crumbled and fell in the distance. Debbie caught a whiff of smoke and something worse. "Where are we?"

"Does it matter? I'm in your arms and we're in my bed. Is there anything more important in all the universe?"

Yes. Debbie blinked. Yes, many things were more important.

A breeze rippled the mosquito netting aside and she saw a devastated city. "Morgan!"

"Shhh, don't look. I'm in Honduras and there's been an earthquake. But don't look at it. Let's just dream a while together."

"We're dreaming?"

He pulled her closer.

"You're a dreamwalker?"

Morgan sighed. "Didn't used to be. Didn't know I could. But I guess I can now. Or you can."

"So you can manipulate me anyway you want to, because we're dreaming."

"No, it's not like that. You want to be here. If you're the dreamwalker, you want to be with me."

"My husband just died. I'm not ready for this."

He gently pushed her onto her back and kissed her. Hunger crept between them, but Debbie shifted and grabbed his hair. "I know you now, General. I won't become a zombie of your Refuge."

"It's not like that."

"You have control of me in this dream. You can make me do anything you wish."

"I want you."

"I want to wake up."

Debbie lurched awake to a sitting position and wiped her sweaty face.

With a grunt of pain, Colonel Morgan Forest rolled off the army cot and fell on the floor of the tent. He was in one of the many emergency medical tent city compounds in Honduras. He was searching for evidence of dark soldiers here, just as he had been in China, then Africa, then Haiti – wherever massive earthquakes had created chaos and children – an inordinate number of them – were missing.

"Everything alright, Colonel?" His tent-mate sat up.

"I thought I was in my own bed and rolled over," he laughed.

"It if had an air conditioner, go back to sleep."

"I'd settle for a cold shower," Morgan grinned. Remnants of an incredible dream still manifested itself.

13 COYOTE

Although no one mentioned where he'd gone or why, Morgan returned on Friday evening, sun-burnt and weary. Saturday, as was the tradition, he threw another cookout. Debbie hadn't planned to go; the idea of a house to herself was tempting, along with the nagging feeling about a bad dream involving Morgan which she couldn't quite remember. But the phone rang Saturday morning just as the children left for Morning Meadow and Morgan thanked her for the cap and its "earth-friendly wrapping."

"Listen, I hate to ask you, but Gabriel has been bragging about a potato salad you make and I was wondering if you'd fix some for tonight's cookout?"

She hemmed and hedged but finally agreed.

After hanging up, she discovered there were no potatoes in her daughter's refrigerator, so she left a note and headed to town on her bike. The bookstore caught her eye – closed this early in the morning, but she took note of the store hours before continuing on to Piggly-Wiggly. She passed a tall thin man in his mid-thirties walking toward the bookstore. He glanced up as she passed him, and for the briefest moment, she thought she was looking into the face of a coyote. It startled her so much, she wobbled on the bike. When she turned to look behind her, he had disappeared.

The same people were at Morgan's. Debbie was swooped inside and lost possession of the huge bowl of potato salad. She discovered it later, after she had been hugged by most everyone present, sitting in the center of the massive picnic table in the back yard, between a casserole of baked beans and something fruity with tiny marshmallows.

She sat beside Hreno on the wicker bench under the tree and pulled out her crochet. The evening passed pleasantly with tales of adventures on alien worlds interspersed with the price changes at the local department store.

She heard her daughter's voice and paid closer attention, "You are so lucky! I loved being pregnant. I always wanted a little girl. I mean, I love my boys more than life, but I'd love to have two girls, too."

Debbie tied another skein onto the end of yarn leading into the sweater she was crocheting and casually suggested, "Seems to me, despite what your gynecologist told you, if you're determined to get pregnant again, you ought to ask Atticus if he'll let you go through a portal."

The women all turned to stare at her.

Morgan asked, "What do you mean?"

"Well, look around. The women who have been through portals are extremely fertile. Every single one of you who is pregnant right now has been through those portals. How many other churches in America have most of their women pregnant all the time?"

The women smiled, as if they were not quite hearing her words, but the polite response was to smile, so they did.

"You can't tell me you haven't thought about it."

Morgan frowned and Becky and Gabriel exchanged worried looks, but no one spoke.

Debbie forged ahead into their silence, getting angry. "I think the more often you go through a portal, the more fertile you become. Ricean rarely goes through a portal now, but when she did travel, as Sword on a different world, she had five children. Visolela never goes through a portal, but Patsy goes through every time one's opened up, to 'hold back the dark' with her songs, and let's face it – two sets of twins and another child in less than five years? So go ahead, Becky, if you want to disregard the danger you'll be putting yourself through by getting pregnant again, but make sure Atticus can help you survive the labor."

For a moment, every face there lost all expression. Their eyes faded in a far-away look of distraction.

Patsy took a step closer, "I declare, I don't know how you come up with this. Look at Debbie," she pointed, addressing the silent group. "She takes one piece of yarn and a hook and before you know it, she's made the cutest little sweater. Isn't that the cutest little thing you've ever seen?"

The women all agreed and the men turned back to their burgers and beer.

Debbie's hands began to shake. Her feet turned to ice. She stared around her in horror. Morgan was grinning, his arm around Gabriel's shoulder, listening to something Le'Vander was saying. He caught her eye, sobered immediately, and was at her side.

"Debbie? What's wrong?" He handed the sweater to Hreno, who tucked it into her bag.

"I'm fine," she mouthed the words, but no sound came out.

"Mom? Mom, what's wrong?" Becky took Hreno's place and Gabriel stood beside Morgan.

"Nothing. Nothing's wrong," she snapped, but the trembling had progressed to her shoulders.

She tried to stand up, to run, to get away from these body snatchers. Her legs obeyed, she pushed against Morgan, and then collapsed.

Debbie was in Morgan's bed. She recognized it as soon as she opened her eyes, but as if from a dream. She had certainly never been in the man's bed before. But the familiarity struck her – white down comforter, mosquito netting pulled behind the head board, and the smell of him, enticing and masculine. Debbie blinked again. She was on top of the comforter with all clothes on except for her shoes. She could hear voices coming from the other side of the door.

"Has she been under a doctor's care?" The voice was deep and accented. It must be the doctor from Africa speaking, she thought.

Her daughter answered. "Not that I know of, but, there's been a lot going on in her life."

"Like what?"

"My father died at Thanksgiving. And she sold everything and moved in with us a month ago."

"It's more than that. Chi is an Elder, Becky. You can confide in him." Morgan's voice sounded deeper than she remembered it.

Becky's voice hardened, "My mother's a very private person."

"If I am to treat her, I should know as much as possible."

Morgan replied, "When Becky's father died, he was bankrupt and had over twenty-seven thousand on credit cards and owed more on his mortgage than the house was worth. Debbie had to sell everything she owned, including most of her clothes, and the bank took the house."

"You make my father sound horrible. It wasn't as simple as all that." Becky always took up for her dad, blindly so.

"He left your mother destitute. I have no sympathy for a man like that," Morgan growled.

Debbie heard her daughter gasp. "Gabriel had no right to tell you those things."

"Your husband didn't say a word, Becky. It's my job to know everything there is about the members and potential members of the Refuge. I know everything there is to know about your mother since she changed her name at sixteen."

"Well, for all your prying into my family's business, you got it wrong. My mother didn't change her name until she married my father when she was nineteen."

"Is everything alright?" Gabriel's calm assurance to the rescue, Debbie thought.

"Your mother-in-law has suffered a severe anxiety attack, brought on by prolonged stress. I would like to run blood work, so please bring her to the clinic before breakfast in the morning."

"Can we take her home?" Becky had calmed.

"She needs quiet. She needs a calm environment. Is she sleeping?"

Gabriel answered, "She has nightmares and wakes up crying."

"To be expected. Bubbles of grief," the doctor replied.

Debbie felt the sorrow erupt from within her soul and was defenseless to its ravages. "Bubbles of grief." That was exactly how her psychologist had described it, all those years ago, before she changed her name when she turned sixteen. She rolled over, smothering her sobs in Morgan's plush pillow.

"Go to church and leave me alone," Debbie growled at her daughter.

"But Dr. Abubakar wants to run blood work on you this morning."

"Mom! Devin took my shoe and won't give it back."

"Cry baby. Here's your stupid shoe!" Something crashed against the wall in the hall.

"The doctor said he wanted me to rest. How is getting up and giving blood and then going to church and eating out resting?"

Thomas yelped again and then both boys stampeded past her bedroom and down the stairs.

Debbie smiled sweetly. "Four hours of peace and quiet would do wonders for me."

"You'll stay in bed?"

"This is a comfortable bed," Debbie side-stepped.

As soon as the car drove away, Debbie got up. She called Rachel, her eldest daughter and asked if she could come stay for a while.

"Well Mom, you know we'd love to have you. But you'd have to sleep on the couch. So, you know, if you wanted to stay a few days, you'd be welcome."

Her youngest daughter answered the phone on the fourth ring, "What?"

"Miriam, it's your mom. Are you alright?"

"We're moving! Can you believe it? We just got settled here a year ago, and they're stationing Paul in Germany. I have three weeks to pack everything up and get all our shots done and I don't know what we're going to do about Paul's daughter. She's starting college this fall. We're going to have to find her an apartment and leave her behind. Of course, her mother will be totally useless, won't lift a finger to help! Typical!"

"I could come help with the packing."

Silence.

"I could come help you pack for the next three weeks."

"That's so sweet of you, Mom, but it's utter chaos here. I just don't think it would be fair to you. I think you need to stay where you are. Once we're settled in Germany, you can come for a visit."

Debbie had no appetite other than for her cup of coffee. It was only ten o'clock. She was exhausted, but restless. She rode slowly to the bookstore and wandered around. A sound, like a harsh barking laugh came from the café. A coyote stood beside a table, laughing with a customer. Debbie blinked. The tall thirty-something man she'd seen earlier wiped off the table; not a coyote.

He glanced at her and smiled. She nodded in return and pulled a book – any book – off the shelf to pretend to lose interest.

Coyote was the Trickster God. Rosa was her best friend growing up in South Dakota. Rosa was Lakota and knew all the stories of her people. She loved to tell about Coyote and they would laugh and laugh deep into the night. They kept in touch after Debbie had been sent into foster care, writing letters every week for years. Rosa married a man from a neighboring tribe because she said that sometimes, when she looked at him, she could see Coyote staring out of his face.

He beat her to death in a drunken rage; she was just twenty-five years old.

Debbie glanced at the book in her hands. *Lakota Myths, as collected by Dr. James Walker.* She smiled sadly and sat in one of the armchairs to re-read this familiar treasure.

Isabel Cortez looked at the open folder on her desk. On one side was a collection of postcards. On the other side, GPS logs. Three years of green dots; the postcard matched the location given by the transistor she'd had implanted in Stelt's buttocks. And now this one red dot. The postcard came from Gatlinburg. The dot was in the middle of Georgia. Probably cow pastures and pecan groves. Not a town for miles.

Cortez tugged on the cuffs of her uniform, coming to a decision. She'd send someone after Stelt. The tracker wouldn't have to meet him, just check. If Stelt's body was buried in a shallow grave, some do-gooder may have posted the card posthumously.

She hoped he wasn't dead. She really wanted to get her hands on that weave. She had such plans for her.

"I guess you had to work again yesterday." Venutha glanced up at John from her table at the bookstore.

"Yeah, these heathen Earthers have no respect for the holy day." He put aside a rag and came over to sit with her. "But I suppose you and your friends went to worship."

"Of course."

"Since I missed it again, why don't you tell me about it?" He sipped from her coffee.

"Sure," Venutha smiled. "Patsy was back; she just had a little boy. And she led the choir in a really beautiful anthem about spires and eagle wings and mountains." Then she rolled her eyes, "Lanza got to sing a solo again."

"You don't like Lanza?"

"I do like her. I like her fine. It's just, well, Wren-at-Dawn likes her a lot. I mean, he can't see anything else except for her."

"Sometimes that can happen when the man is young and the woman is pretty. Is she pretty?"

"She's beautiful! She has almond skin and blue eyes and white hair and big boobs."

"What?" John scowled.

Venutha reddened and said, "And Atticus taught about encouragement and support through times of trouble."

"Hmm," John hummed. "Was everyone there? All your litter mates?"

"Oh sure. Jeremy and Hreno, and I already mentioned Wren-at-Dawn. And Dad and Papa are back, and Eserno brought a townie with her and he's going to pray with Atticus."

"Will they dance at Winter's Night, do you think?"

"Eserno?" Venutha's heart pattered at the thought that John might have meant Wren-at-Dawn and Lanza.

"Will they wed?"

"Oh. I don't know. Eserno's my age. But I guess she could."

"On my world, girls get married as soon as they can bear children."

Venutha saw a shadow pass over his features. "Are you married?"

"I used to be. My wife died and my daughter was stolen from me."

Venutha put her hand over his. "I'm so sorry."

Tears sprang to his eyes and her innocent kindness flowed into him. He forced the grief back down, swallowing it like bile, refusing the balm of comfort. "What are your friends doing today?"

"Wren-at-Dawn and Pierre are looking at some pasture land for sale. Jeremy is spending the day in Ben's operating room, helping him."

"And your other litter mate, Hreno?"

"She's learning how to crochet. She made me a cap and it's really pretty."

"What's crochet?"

"It's like weaving, but just one hook."

"Weave? Hreno's weaving?"

"No, not like," Venutha lowered her voice. "How do you know about weaving?"

John was scowling, upset with himself for revealing too much. "My aunt used to weave fishing nets."

"Oh, well then. Crochet is like making fishing nets."

"She made you a cap?"

"Yes. And now she's making a blanket. It's really pretty, too."

"She's your best friend. Didn't you want to be with her and learn this crochet, too?"

"We don't have to be together twenty-four--seven." Venutha pouted. "Sometimes, a girl just needs –"

John glowered.

"Well, I don't know what it is, but sometimes, I just need to leave the Ranch and the Refuge behind."

"But Hreno doesn't?"

"No, I don't think so. She is fascinated by Grandma Debbie's crochet. And she gets along with all the other church women. She loves babies."

"And what?"

"She fits in. She belongs." *She wasn't born in a barn,* Venutha thought. "And she's pretty. Everyone says so, even Wren-at-Dawn."

"The horseman who likes Lanza?"

"Yeah."

John got up to make a coffee and bagel for a patron, but he looked angry. Venutha heard the church bells and jumped up. Waving at John, she hurried out of the store.

14 YOU DOING OK?

"She's up to something." Wren-at-Dawn swung his cane pole and watched the baited hook skip across the stream's surface and then slowly sink into the rippling water.

Pierre raised one eyebrow.

"She's being nice."

Pierre's lips twitched.

"And she isn't wearing those silly clothes as much anymore. You know, she loved those ruffly short shorts and her shirts don't show her tummy anymore."

Pierre nodded.

"And she reads books. Every time she has free time, she pulls out a book, and," Wren-at-Dawn paused.

"And what?"

"And she ignores the rest of us."

"Could it be that the queen is growing up?"

"We all are."

Pierre smiled, "I reckon you are."

"You have discussed it with Venutha, right?" Joan was bathing Baby Ben. Her husband was helping, sort of.

"I wouldn't use the word 'discuss'. It was more a chat."

"A chat?"

"Sure."

"How many words?"

Ben looked up at the ceiling. "Three?"

"You summed up sex and menstruation in three words?"

"Yeah."

"What were they?"

"'You doing OK?'"

"Ben, I swear. She's your daughter and she's going into puberty. She knows more about dogs and horses than she does about humans. And I don't know if you noticed, but dogs and horses have a different view on abstinence and pregnancy than humans do."

"Yeah, well," Ben frowned. "Are you sure she's old enough to discuss this?"

Joan was about to yell, and then saw her beloved man was serious. He didn't want his little girl to grow up. So she laughed and hugged him. "I love you."

"Yeah?"

"Yeah."

Hreno snuck up behind Jeremy. He was standing with one foot on the rails of the back fence, watching the newer dog guards running with the pack. One little boy cart-wheeled along while his puppy dashed through his legs and arms in perfect rhythm. A new girl was using hand signals with her dog. Hreno grinned and pounced on Jeremy, pulling a crocheted cap onto his head.

He turned, startled. Her mouth flew open; he had tears on his face. She took a step back. "I made you a cap. To keep you safe." She spoke barely above a whisper. "And warm."

He wiped at his cheeks and pulled the cap off, looking at it. "It's nice. Thanks."

"I'm making a blanket now. Only Grandmother Debbie calls it an afghan."

Jeremy nodded, glancing back at the dogs.

"If you want, I'll make you one, too. To keep you warm at night."

His face darkened and she knew it had been the wrong thing to say; Magyar used to keep him warm at night.

"Are you going swimming this afternoon? Some of us are going to the pool."

"No." He rolled the cap between his hands. "This is real soft."

Hreno nodded.

"That beagle's boy needs to be firmer. He spoils the dog. Won't be ready for battle, if it comes to it."

"Beagles don't fight well, anyway. Or that's what Venutha says. They sure make a lot of noise, though."

"Like Venutha," Jeremy laughed.

"Remember when Patsy kicked her out of the choir?" Hreno was pleased she'd gotten Jeremy to smile.

He pointed, "That young coon dog sounds better than Venutha singing."

"Yeah," Hreno readily agreed. "Wouldn't it be something if you could teach the dogs to sing with the light?"

Jeremy blinked. "That's an idea. I bet I could."

"I'm sure you could." Hreno's eyes shown with assurance.

Jeremy grinned and nodded. "Yeah. That might just be something."

Hreno tilted her head back, "Howl –lelujah!"

Jeremy joined her in a mock of Handel's famous chorus, "Howl-lelujah!"

From his concealed position in the oak tree next to the road, aided by ingenious binoculars, Stelt watched his daughter. She looked happy. And she was behaving like a good girl. When she threw her head back and laughed, Stelt smiled. She was happy. She had good friends. She was beautiful. She hadn't turned to despair.

Then the young man hugged his daughter. She snatched back the cap she'd given him and ran away. The boy chased her; they were both laughing and chasing each other, playing for possession of the cap.

The cap the weave taught her to make. The weave who'd come into the bookstore. Venutha had called her Grandma Debbie. She had no right, teaching his daughter to weave gifts for men.

He'd have to think about redeeming that woman.

"I tell you, Ohamaha, it was just weird." Venutha sat beside her dog and let the puppies crawl over her. "They sat next to each other and held hands and looked like they were going to tell me something horrible."

"I don't understand why they felt they needed to discuss it with you. You were raised by horses."

"But, that's the weird part. They kept repeating that horses and dogs don't marry each other."

"I beg your pardon. Of course we do. I'm married to Gamga."

"I explained that. So then they said that dogs can have puppies and horses can have colts but humans should be married first."

"That is weird. What does marriage have to do with having puppies?"

"I don't know. Dad just started shouting that I was not to even think about having puppies before I got married. And Mom started laughing."

"Humans," Ohamaha nosed the runt toward an empty teat. "I love you dearly, Venutha, but I do not understand humans."

Friday afternoon, Venutha rode Startles-Pheasants to the bookstore.

"This isn't Patsy's house."

"I know," Venutha answered the horse. "I just need to go inside for a minute. I'll be right back out."

"Well, what am I supposed to do?"

"Just," Venutha straightened her hair and brushed off her jeans. "Stand there. I'll be right back."

"Just stand here."

"Yes! I'll be right back!" Venutha tried not to dash into the café, but John was grinning at her.

"Nice horse."

"Her name's Startles-Pheasants."

Venutha put both hands on the counter between them. "We're having a picnic. Everybody at the Ranch. We're going to have a fish fry and baked chicken and biscuits. The picnic is tomorrow. And I want you to come."

John nodded, mulled it over seriously, and said, "I won't be here tomorrow."

"You're leaving?"

John's fingertips touched Venutha's on the counter. "Not for good. Just a day or two."

"Oh."

"But," John leaned forward. "I'm not leaving until tomorrow. I'm going dancing tonight. If you wanted to, you could come with me."

Venutha beamed and then her face fell. "I have to babysit for Patsy and Le'Vander. And they will be out until ten o'clock at the earliest."

"Well, that's settled then. You go sit on the babies and meet me here when you get through."

"The store closes at nine."

"The parking lot doesn't. I'll be waiting for you in a car."

"What kind of car?"

"I haven't decided yet." He grinned. "It'll be the only one there. And if I'm not the one driving, don't get in."

Venutha was thrilled. "Yes. I'll see you at ten."

"See you, girly." John patted her hand.

Venutha floated out the door, not noticing Debbie seated at the nearby couch. Debbie had overheard most of the conversation and wasn't sure what to do. The man was obviously decades older than Venutha, but the Refuge seemed to encourage young girls to get married early. Not child-brides, which was considered an abomination. Just really young. Her left shoulder was killing her; sometimes it did that. The scar from an injury she'd had when she was about Venutha's age burned like ice right now. Sometimes it just tingled. No reason for it, other than cut tendons that didn't heal cleanly. She put down the new yarn and massaged the ache.

She felt someone staring. Glancing sideways, she saw a coyote pacing in front of the counter in the café. She blinked, and the coyote became the man whose name tag read John. He cocked his head and watched her approach.

"You want something?"

Debbie took a steadying breath. "I don't know you and you don't know me, but I do know that child Venutha. She's sweet and innocent."

"Yes," the man nodded. "She's a good girl."

"You may think it's none of my business, but I'm making it my business. If you do anything to change her from being sweet, innocent, and good, you're going to answer to me. And I am neither sweet, innocent, nor good."

Stelt blinked. She was a powerful weave; as a redecmer, he could sense them instinctively. And here she was, threatening him, protecting the little innocent Venutha.

"You're teaching Hreno to crochet."

Debbie frowned at the sudden shift in thought. "Yes."

He nodded. "Good. I didn't think it was good at first, you teaching girls to make things to give away to boys. But now, I see you want to keep her safe. So, here I stand. I will never cause harm to Venutha, this I swear on my lord. Venutha reminds me of

71

my daughter. My wife was killed and my daughter was stolen. I think you understand grief and sorrow and loss."

Debbie was cautious. Her husband used to sound just as convincing. The deeper the lie, the more convincing the details.

"You may see her as a daughter-figure, but that's not how she sees you. So don't take advantage of her, or you'll live to regret it." Debbie turned gracefully and went back to pick up her crochet bag on the couch.

"They call you Grandmother Spider, like in Morning Meadow," he called across the café.

"Yes."

"They call me John."

Debbie focused on him, trying to ignore how much he looked of coyote. It was no use. No matter how she tried, she distrusted this man instinctively.

"Hey Mom," Gabriel stuck his head in the door. "You ready?"

"John, this is my son-in-law Gabriel Igelsias. He's the sheriff."

"Howdy, Sheriff." John smiled openly.

"Hi," Gabriel nodded.

"You take care now, Grandmother Spider."

"You take care, too." She almost said 'Coyote. '

Gabriel frowned in confusion. Debbie was being almost rude in response to the café guy's friendliness. But, she was going through a tough time.

Venutha read to the five darlings of Patsy and Le'Vander, fed them, bathed them, and then put them to bed.

She examined herself in the mirror and liked what she saw. She'd been to dances at the Refuge, and the Ranch had them every season. And of course, there was Winter's Eve, where the last dance is reserved for those who want to get married. She wished she had on a skirt or dress – something that swirled, but her jeans and shirt would do. She expertly applied make-up – she'd seen Patsy do so enough times. She nodded at herself and then stuck her tongue out. "So there, Jeremy."

She spent the next two hours reading and watching the clock. She also practiced what she would tell Le'Vander, so he wouldn't drive her home. She'd sent Startles-Pheasants back by herself as soon as she'd arrived – Patsy didn't like the benefits horses usually left in her yard due to her house still being used as a beauty parlor. Venutha knew she was not good at lying, so she decided to stick as closely to the truth as possible. She qualified her decision on three things. 1. Her parents had never told her she couldn't date; dating was what Earthers did. 2. They'd never said she couldn't go dancing. 3. They didn't say she had to go straight home after babysitting.

Her parents would be easy to deal with. Patsy would be all giggly about her dating. But Le'Vander seemed to know a whole lot more than he ever let on.

The closer it got to ten o'clock, the worse her stomach felt. When she heard the key turning in the lock, her mouth went dry and her ears burned.

They were all smoochy with each other. Patsy ran upstairs to check on the children and Le'Vander handed her a ten dollar bill. She didn't actually charge for babysitting, so it was more a tip than a payment.

"Thanks, Le'Vander. I'm glad you and Patsy had such a nice time. I tell you, little Levi acts just like you every chance he gets. 'My pa this' and 'My pa that. ' Well, good night!" She opened the back door.

"Where are you going? Don't you need me to drive you home?"

"Oh, no. My date will drive me home. I have a date. With a friend. And he – my date – will drive me home. After our date."

Le'Vander tilted his head. "Is he picking you up from here?"

"No. He works at the bookstore. I'll meet him there."

"It's ten-fifteen. I don't like the idea of you walking alone at night."

"Well, you could drive me to the bookstore, but it's just a couple blocks away."

"Patsy," he hollered up the stairs. "I'm driving Venutha to meet her date at the bookstore. I'll be back."

Venutha smiled, but her stomach burned.

There was only one car in the parking lot. Its motor was running but its headlights were off. Le'Vander pulled in and shut off the engine. "You sure that's him?"

"Yes, I'm sure." She fumbled, trying to get out of the van. "Thanks!"

"Do your parents know about this?"

Venutha was glad it was dark because she felt her cheeks burn. Mimicking Patsy, she exclaimed, "Le'Vander! What do you take me for?"

She slammed the door and all but ran to the bright red Chrysler LeBarron convertible and got in.

"Who was that man?"

"Everyone knows Le'Vander," She said, breathless. "I baby sat his five children tonight."

John peered up at the driver in the van, glaring. Le'Vander glared back.

"Go. Let's go," Venutha whispered.

John flipped on the lights and cautiously backed the car around the van and out onto the street.

Le'Vander counted to ten, and then pulled out his cell phone. He drove, a block behind the LeBarron, and waited for Ben to answer the phone.

"Doctor Ben's office," Jeremy answered.

"Hey, it's Le'Vander. Let me talk to Ben."

"He's – um – he and Joan are – well, Le'Vander, it's late and they're busy. OK?" Jeremy felt his cheeks burn.

"Oh. Well." Le'Vander thought better than to disturb him. "Is this Wren-at-Dawn?"

"No, it's Jeremy. Wren-at-Dawn's gone to bed, I think."

"Is Pierre around?"

"No. He's in Atlanta, at a horse auction. Is everything OK? Venutha was supposed to be at your house. Is something wrong?"

"I'm probably being stupid, but – do you know if Venutha had a date tonight?"

"The queen? She's just a baby!"

"Hmm."

"Who's she with?"

"Some guy. She says he works at the bookstore. She had me drop her off. He's old enough to drive a car, but I couldn't see his face. Well, this ain't right."

"What?"

"He just pulled into the Red Bird Tavern. I know Venutha's too young to go bar-hopping."

"The old place off the highway?"

"Yep."

Jeremy's mind leaped into realms of heroic possibilities. "Thanks, Le'Vander. Here's Dad. I'll tell him and we'll be right there."

"You want me to go get her for you?"

"No. No reason to embarrass the little princess. We'll just be real quiet about it. But thanks. And Le'Vander? Do you mind not telling anyone?"

"Well, sure. OK, if Ben will be right here."

"Absolutely," Jeremy lied.

Jeremy hung up and raced into the bunkhouse. He tapped Wren-at-Dawn on the shoulder and put his finger over his lips. He gestured him to follow and was saddling Symetaur when Wren-at-Dawn walked in, still pulling a shirt over his head.

The stench of cigarette smoke made Venutha's eyes water. John had her by the elbow and pushed her firmly toward the bar. They perched on wooden stools with cracked plastic covers and Venutha gaped at her surroundings.

The lights were low, with spotlights scattered incongruously around. Men and women sat at tables, booths, and the bar. The noise was tremendous. A band – two guitars, a keyboard, and a woman in a black dress – were on a little stage, warming up. The center of the tavern was covered by a wooden floor.

Le'Vander walked in and looked around. He saw Venutha at the bar with the man and recognized a few people around the place. He heard a belch and then a guffaw he would never forget and headed in that direction. "Hey Beucephalas. Mind if I join you?"

Big B glanced up and grinned. "Pull up a chair, little brother. You must be plumb tuckered out. Let me buy you a beer."

"Thanks," Le'Vander kept his eyes on Venutha and her date.

"Whiskey," John ordered. "And bottled water."

The barkeep glanced at Venutha, who gave him a chirrupy grin.

The lights dimmed further and the woman walked up to the mike.

"Here we go, girl." He slung back the shot of amber fire and grabbed her hand.

The woman's voice was awful but the beat of the song and the flashing lights, cigarette smoke, strangers, and John's dominance swirled around Venutha. They began with a line dance; Venutha easily caught on to the steps. The band played for thirty minutes while John and Venutha danced: line, two step, Texas waltz, and back to line.

During the third dance of the first set, Jeremy and Wren-at-Dawn ambled in and quickly took an empty booth.

"Do you see her?" Jeremy asked.

"I'm looking."

"Get you boys something?" The waitress might have been Joan's age, but she had on so much make-up, it was hard to tell. The skin above her full breasts was crinkly with sun-abuse and there were dollar bills peeking out from her cleavage. Her cut-off jean shorts showed an inch of her bottom above her thighs as she side-stepped men walking behind her. One slipped two fingers along the exposed cheek. The waitress grimaced and then smiled a fake smile at him as he tucked a dollar bill in with the others.

Jeremy was afraid Wren-at-Dawn was about to do something noble, so he shouted, "Two bottled waters."

She looked at them, gauging their ages accurately, "Sure, honey."

As she left, she earned dollar tips from several men along her path back to the bar. One of the tippers was Beaucephus.

"Hey Le'Vander," the waitress stopped. "I haven't seen you in a dog's age. How you?"

"Blessed, I'm just blessed, Tracy. How have you been?"

"Missing you." The men around her slapped the table and laughed rudely. "I can't get that damned lawn mower to cut straight to save my life. I don't suppose you have a minute this week to drop by?"

"I'll see what I can do, Tracy. Say," he nodded at the horsemen. "See those two boys yonder? They're friends of mine. We're here making sure their little sister don't get into trouble. But their daddy was supposed to walk in with them. Since he's not here, I reckon they're going to do something manly and heroic."

Tracy grinned. "Damn! Don't you just hate it when they get all manly and heroic!"

"See the little girl with that man over there?"

"John Parker? Yeah, I know him."

"What do you know about him?"

"Never tips and only ever drinks whiskey and dances. That man loves to dance. That's about it. Listen, I got to fill some orders here or Red will start yelling. I'll keep an eye on them, make sure he don't slip nothing in her drink. That OK?"

"Yeah, thanks."

"I sure hope Patsy knows what she's got. There is none better than you, Le'Vander." She walked away and swatted at the next man who tried to tip her.

"Do you have any money?" Jeremy asked.

"No, why?"

Jeremy rolled his eyes and pulled out his wallet.

"There." Wren-at-Dawn pointed.

They watched as Venutha and a man danced a slow waltz around the floor. Venutha was beaming up at him as he said something.

"He's old! He's really old!" Jeremy growled. "He must be at least thirty-five!"

Wren-at-Dawn schooled his features to be Pierre-like-calm.

"Do you know him? I think I've seen him before, but I can't remember where."

"I don't know him, but there is something dark about him. Can't you feel it?" Wren-at-Dawn fingered the scar he received when his father had tried to redeem him six years earlier. It itched, like a healing wound.

The music ended and the man led Venutha by the hand back to the bar where she gulped down a bottle of water, laughing along with the man who drank something out of a shot glass.

"So, how should we play this?" Jeremy handed the waitress the amount she stated, plus an extra two dollars. "You could distract him and I'll grab Venutha."

"She's not doing anything wrong. She looks," he almost said 'beautiful.' "Happy."

"But we came to," Jeremy almost said 'rescue her'. "Bring her home."

"We will. Just – be patient. We need to watch this guy; learn more about the way he fights, before we confront him."

"You don't suppose, he's not one of us?"

Venutha laughed at something and put her hand on the man's arm. He covered her hand with his.

The band started up again and the man dragged Venutha onto the floor. Le'Vander left his brother's table and walked over to the boys. "I'm going to assume Ben is out in the truck."

"Hey, Le'Vander," Jeremy reddened. "He – Ben's-"

Wren-at-Dawn stated, "We didn't tell him. We'll watch her."

"You boys have no business being here, and neither does Venutha. I'm going outside to make a phone call to Patsy. Then I'm coming back in and we're all going to go home."

"We were just about to leave. We just wanted Venutha to have a nice time first."

Le'Vander squinted in warning at Wren-at-Dawn and walked away.

"She's good. I didn't know she could dance."

"We used to – she used to dance a lot, when we were kids." Wren-at-Dawn watched as the man twirled her around and back again. They did a fast two-step as the bad singer tried to keep up with the musicians.

The more they danced, the more uncomfortable Wren-at-Dawn became. Finally, after that set ended and Venutha flounced back toward the bar, Wren-at-Dawn felt like he was going to explode. But he looked like he was calm.

As they passed a table of men, Beaucephus cupped his mouth and pretended to sneeze: "Jail bait!"

The men around him chuckled unpleasantly.

"What that mean? Jail bait?" the man with Venutha halted, glaring at the townie.

Beaucephus rolled his eyes at his friends.

"I asked you a question, Earther."

"He is one of us," Jeremy whispered.

Wren-at-Dawn stood. "You don't have to be one of us to be from another world."

Across the room, Big B stood, "Earther? Who you calling Earther? My name's Big B. Beaucephus McAfee. You best be remembering my name now."

His companion grabbed his wrist. "He's one of those refugees. Be careful."

Another friend grunted, "Yeah, they're some kind of secret militia. I hear they train their children to fight."

"Is that right? You one of them Refugees?" Le'Vander's brother swayed in his inebriated state.

Venutha tugged John's sleeve. "It's alright. Let's go sit down."

"Yeah, take your little jail bait and go sit down. But not here. This here bar is for red-blooded Americans. Not some damn refugees off the reservation."

John moved swiftly. Pushing Venutha behind him with one hand, he slammed his other fist into Big B's face.

His companions leapt to their feet with shouts.

Wren-at-Dawn took Venutha's arm on one side and Jeremy took the other. She yelped.

John ducked under Beaucephus' wide swing. Big B's nose was broken and bloody and he bellowed in fury. Two more swift punches from John and Big B was on the floor. His companions were hesitant in the face of John's savagery.

"Hey you!" Red the bartender yelled. "Get out! And take your kids with you."

John looked at Venutha and recognized the boys holding her arms as her littermates.

"Yeah, get out," the man speaking was helping his friend off the floor.

"Damn refugees," someone growled.

Wren-at-Dawn glared at John and fought the urge to scratch his scar.

"Let's go," Venutha insisted. She took John's bloody hand and, still being held by the boys, walked backward out of the bar.

In the steamy Georgia night, the four of them stopped. No one said anything for ten seconds. Venutha, because she couldn't decide how to react – anger or embarrassment. Wren-at-Dawn, because he had seen how quickly and viciously this man fought. Jeremy, because he was so excited about rescuing a damsel in distress in the middle of a real bar fight. John, because he knew that one of the men before him was a weave and the other one had dared to hug his daughter.

The horses walked up to them. Le'Vander watched them from his truck – cellphone to his ear -- but didn't interrupt.

Wren-at-Dawn took a step in front of Venutha and addressed the stranger. "Whom do you serve?"

John took a deep breath. He could use this incident to his advantage, if he played it just right. He pasted on a grin he knew made him look harmless and homey. "I serve anyone who wants a cup of coffee. I don't fight anymore."

"You just fought that man."

"Yeah, well, he made a rude remark about your sister. That's not to be tolerated on any world."

"Sister?" Jeremy asked.

"Sure. You're Jeremy, and you're Wren-at-Dawn, Venutha's litter mates. She's told me all about you. You're the world's greatest horseman and you're going to be the world's greatest animal doctor. Well, second greatest. Ain't no one going to be better than her daddy, am I right?"

The boys blinked and Venutha grinned.

He stuck out his hand to Jeremy first. "They call me John Parker."

The teen automatically shook his hand. "Don't I know you?"

"You do now."

"No, it's just, you look so familiar somehow."

"I've been around."

"He goes to church with us," Venutha volunteered.

He turned to Wren-at-Dawn and held out his hand.

"Whom do you serve?" Wren-at-Dawn's voice was unswayable.

Tougher than he looks, Stelt realized. He shifted into a slippery honesty. "I don't. Not anymore. Not after they killed my wife and stole my daughter. I came through with the other refugees, but when Atticus said I'd have to go back, I knew I'd turn to despair if I went back to my empty farm. So I stayed here."

Wren-at-Dawn kept frowning, so John dropped his hand and sighed deeply. "It's not always a choice of light and dark, good and evil. As a matter of fact, most of the worlds just choose to be gray." He shrugged, "But you two, look at you. Coming to protect your sister. Men of honor. Venutha was right about you. You shine with the light, just like her. You shame me for my mediocrity. But my heart was broken. You know all about how that feels, I know you men do."

The boys stiffened, but Venutha got teary-eyed.

"Venutha is a good girl. She'd make any father or brother proud. And I'm proud that she befriended me. It makes me think that maybe, one day, I'll serve the light again."

"You could pray with Atticus," Venutha suggested.

"Now, why would he want to waste time with the likes of me?" John did the *gosh-golly grin* that usually worked. "Well, I had a wonderful time, Venutha. I guess you're safe enough in your brothers' care, so I'll let them take you home. It was an honor to meet you, Horseman of Atticus. And you, Veterinarian of Atticus."

Venutha beamed at him, "Good night, John. Thanks!"

They watched him saunter off towards a red Le Baron convertible.

"Nice car," Jeremy said.

"What do you think you're doing here?" Fists on hips, she turned on them.

"Listening to music. Having a drink," Wren-at-Dawn replied. "Why?"

Jeremy watched in amazement as Venutha blinked and lowered her arms.

"Well, we're heading back home. Do you want a ride?"

Venutha was surprised that she felt so disappointed. Wren-at-Dawn acted like he didn't care that she was there. "Yeah. Thanks."

She rode behind Jeremy on Wild Willow. When they got to the barn, no one spoke as they settled the horses back into their stalls.

"Well, good night," she said hesitantly.

"Yeah. OK." Wren-at-Dawn nodded with his back to her. "Jeremy needs to check on Ohamaha. You might as well walk across with him."

Jeremy blinked, but quickly took up the lie. "Sure. Thanks."

Frogs filled the air with their singing as they walked.

"You're a good dancer."

"You think so?" she smiled.

"Yeah. Could you teach me how?"

"Sure. I think so."

"You know, Ben wouldn't be happy that you were in a bar tonight."

Venutha didn't say anything.

"You might want to put your clothes straight into the washing machine. Cigarette smoke stinks."

"Oh. I will." She walked up the steps. "So, you two were just there. Just at the bar, like for no special reason?"

Jeremy tried not to grin. "We like the music. And," inspired, he lied, "the girls are hot there."

"I hadn't noticed." From her place by the back door, she could see Wren-at-Dawn standing at the stable door, watching.

"Good night."

"I thought you were going to check on Ohamaha."

"I think she'll be OK. I don't want to wake her puppies. You need to get the runt to eat a little bit more. I'll ask the cooks to make some especially soft food for him." Jeremy felt like a god. He'd rescued a damsel in distress, been in a bar fight, and now was protecting the Queen and she didn't even realize it, like a secret agent. He bowed, "Good night, your majesty."

She giggled. When he stood up, she kissed his cheek. "Night."

15 THE WAYSTATION

Horses, dogs and humans roamed around the five acres of pastureland. There were another thirty-five acres attached to the property, but the farther fields had grown wild. Pierre pointed as he walked with Ben, Joan, Jeremy, Wren-at-Dawn, Lanza, Venutha and Hreno. "There's a stand of crabapples and peaches over there. And the silo is still useable. The farmer rotated his crops every three years so peanuts are in that acre, corn there, and tomatoes and bell peppers there."

"The horses will love that," Jeremy said.

"We'll keep the same crops rotating, and the fourth acre over there lies fallow," Wren-at-Dawn added as Lanza swung their joined hands, smiling.

"There's no shelter for the horses," Venutha snapped, her eyes locked on the couple's entwined fingers.

Pierre explained, "Barn blew over years back, but the foundation is still solid cement and stone. Matt is going to send a bulldozer next week to clear the debris, once Venutha and Jeremy make sure there's no nests or boroughs in the mess."

"We saw some feral cats," Wren-at-Dawn said.

"Cats? Like kittens? Eduviges has those!" Lanza beamed at the horseman, seemingly oblivious to everyone else around her.

"Cats?" Jeremy grinned at Venutha. She grabbed his hand and they ran together to explore the debris.

"Speaking of Eduviges," Joan spoke firmly. "She said she needs to speak with you about an anthem you and she will be performing. I see her over there, beside Patsy. This would be as good a time as any. Wren-at-Dawn can join you later."

"I have all afternoon to spend with Wren-at-Dawn. Eduviges can wait."

Wren-at-Dawn hung his head and his ears turned red.

Pierre looked at Lanza without smiling. Ben looked anywhere but at the girl.

"Oh. Perhaps I will go and speak with Eduviges. If you'll excuse me," Lanza curtsied graciously. Then she cupped Wren-at-Dawn's cheek in her free hand and kissed his lips delicately. She grinned as she walked away, releasing his hand only at the last moment.

They began to walk slowly, in deference to Pierre's knee and Joan's pregnancy.

Hreno smiled up at Wren-at-Dawn who was looking behind them at Lanza. She took his hand. He glanced at her, surprised, and then smiled back.

When they finally reached the barn, Venutha grabbed Hreno and dragged her to a pile of timbers and weeds. "Look, there are eight kittens in there. The momma grabbed one and ran off that way."

"We explained to her that she wasn't in danger. But you know cats," Jeremy laughed.

"We'll come back Monday and gather them up safely." Wren-at-Dawn suggested.

"Not Monday," both Hreno and Venutha said together.

Wren-at-Dawn scowled. "Tuesday then. The sooner we can clear the barn, the sooner we can rebuild it."

"What about the house?"

"I'm glad you asked, Venutha."

"Are you, Poppa Pierre?"

"Indeedy I am. Here's the key. You four go open it up and start exploring. We'll join up momentarily."

Wren-at-Dawn took the key and they dashed across the yard to the two-story wooden antebellum with a rusted tin roof.

"I don't like it," Joan said once they were out of earshot. "They're too young."

"And how old were they during the Battle of Crystal Lake? And all the other battles since then?"

Joan glared at Pierre and made that smacking noise the men so disliked but hadn't heard in a while.

"It'll be like summer camp for them," Ben suggested, shifting his son onto the other hip.

"You obviously didn't go to the same summer camps I did," she speared her husband with an unhappy look.

Inside, Wren-at-Dawn walked with Jeremy while the girls squealed and ran from room to room. "The front parlor has French doors which open onto the side porch. You can stand there and see all the fields. The kitchen is small. When the house was built, the kitchen was in a separate building out back. The formal dining room needs a new floor, so don't go in there. The bathrooms were added onto the back porch up and down stairs."

"Look at this bath tub!" Hreno yelled.

"We could swim in it," Venutha giggled.

Hreno shrieked and the girls dashed past the boys.

"Why?" Jeremy had his hands over his ears and slowly removed them. "Why do girls do that?"

"Look at this stairway!" Venutha yelled, her voice echoing up and back.

"Be careful! Some of the boards have rotted."

"Yes, Wren-at-Dawn," Hreno giggled.

The boys exchanged looks.

Venutha leaned over the banister above them. "Come on! You've got to see this!"

The stairs opened into a square surrounding an open balcony overlooking the stairwell.

"Pierre said this helps the hot air swirl up and out of the vents in the roof."

"Well, AC wouldn't hurt." Jeremy glanced around. "Where are the light switches?"

"There aren't any," Wren-at-Dawn said. "No electricity. We're off the grid here."

Hreno paled. "Like other worlds. Earth's the only place I've been to with electricity."

Wren-at-Dawn nodded.

Five doors lined the square. Venutha pushed one open. The large bright room with a broken window was empty.

"This is pretty." There was a door in the center of the left wall which opened into an identical bedroom. They exited back into the hall. The next door directly in front of the stairs opened onto the back porch, which ran the entire width of the backside of the house, and the bathroom.

"It's a sleeping porch." Wren-at-Dawn pointed. "Hammocks used to hang from these eye-hooks and it used to be completely screened in."

"Twelve," Venutha stated. "Big enough for a dozen hammocks."

"Bathroom's small," Hreno pulled aside the faded calico curtain separating the sleeping porch from a sink, toilet, and small iron-clad bath tub.

"This is like an upstairs bunkhouse," Jeremy walked to the torn and tattered screen. "You can see the highway over there, I think."

Venutha led them back into the upstairs landing, continuing to the next room.

"Wow, this is huge!" Hreno exclaimed. "We could all sleep in here."

"What's this?" Venutha pushed open a door next to the fireplace that led into a tiny room. "Is this a closet?"

Wren-at-Dawn stood behind her, looking in. "It's a nursery. All the other doors open onto the landing. Not a safe thing for crawling infants."

"A nursery? Let me see," Hreno pushed Wren-at-Dawn against Venutha and looked in. "The window is high up, too, not huge like the other rooms. So the baby couldn't accidently fall over the sill."

Venutha's heart raced. She couldn't breathe well. The familiar scent of Wren-at-Dawn seemed overwhelming, dominating suddenly. There was space for her to walk into the nursery, but she would have had to walk away from the feel of his chest pressing against her shoulders. She looked up; he was staring at her. But it made her stomach flutter.

Jeremy shoved against Hreno, "Get in or get out. Let me see."

Venutha opened the door opposite and a cool breeze flowed between the bedrooms through the nursery.

Hreno pointed at four marks on the floor under the window. "Look, I bet that's where the crib stood. That's where I'd put one."

"And the rocking chair should go here," Jeremy stood next to the imaginary crib. "When I have kids, I'm going to rock them to sleep every night."

Venutha giggled.

"Don't laugh, your majesty," he bowed. "There's a guy, used to be a friend of mine in school. He's a year younger than me and he already has a baby. A little girl."

"My dad said women get married on our world the Winter Dance after their first menstruation," Hreno blinked in surprise at herself. She hadn't mentioned her father in years.

"John says the same thing about his homeworld."

Beside her, Wren-at-Dawn stiffened.

Hreno continued, "There's something sad about an empty nursery."

Jeremy looked at Hreno and his cheeks turned red. She must have felt him staring, because she glanced at him and laughed.

"Anybody home?" Ben yelled from downstairs.

"We're up here. We'll come down," Wren-at-Dawn called.

They all sat on the steps or on the porch in ancient rocking chairs which had been left behind.

"Well," Ben started. "What do you think?"

"It's sweet," Hreno smiled.

"It could use electricity," Jeremy added.

Venutha drew a deep breath, "It's perfect. It will make an excellent waystation for the horsemen and dog guards."

Pierre grinned and tucked his chin. Ben looked shocked and Joan suspicious.

"That's what Atticus needs, isn't it? A place to send away our packs. Send them to hold back the dark on other worlds."

"Honey," Ben began.

Venutha held up a hand. "I'm not stupid. And I'm not a little girl anymore."

Pierre whistled softly, calming Venutha as he would a wild mustang.

Wren-at-Dawn spoke softly, "It's why we've been training them. It's why they came here."

Hreno looked at Jeremy, who shrugged.

Venutha brushed at a fly, "I know that."

"We'll use this plantation for training at first. We'll get the house repaired and the barn built, plus we'll put in a state of the art surgery with a generator. Then we'll bring small packs here with their humans for field trips to visit other worlds." Ben smiled, "Just like summer camp."

Joan rolled her eyes.

Pierre continued, "I reckon four years before we need to start saying good byes."

"And it won't be good bye. Just 'see you soon'," Ben said.

"Like with Otka," Joan added.

"And," Wren-at-Dawn pushed his shoulder against Venutha's. "Speaking of Otka; Jeremy asked why we are off the grid."

Jeremy leaped to a conclusion, "Dragons can't fly near power lines."

Venutha looked into Wren-at-Dawn's face. He smiled and gently bumped against her shoulder again.

Hreno shrieked and leaped off the porch. "Dragons! We're going to have dragons here!" She ran back and yanked Venutha off the porch. The girls did an energetic dance of some kind, full of joy.

"So, you'll need two weaves to open a portal large enough for dragons."

"Yes, Jeremy. And a vet who can speak with any animal who comes through."

Jeremy gaped at Ben. "Me? I get to live here?"

"If you want," Pierre nodded.

Jeremy flung himself off the porch and joined the girls dancing.

"It was a good idea, Wren-at-Dawn," Pierre patted his shoulder. "The more dragons we can bring through the portals and send them back healthy, the better chance they'll have of not becoming extinct."

"Thanks, Papa."

"And by having the dogs and horses rotate through here, no one will realize its true purpose; to help dragons procreate."

"You really think the portals cause it?" Joan asked.

"Sweet pea, something else causes it."

She rolled her eyes at her husband, blushing.

"But Atticus is certain that fertility is linked to the portals somehow," Ben said. "If no dragon has laid an egg in half a century, this may save them."

"So, this will be more than a waystation." Wren-at-Dawn grinned. "It'll be a honeymoon hotel for dragons."

"Lord-have-mercy," Pierre moaned. "Don't let Otka hear you call it that."

They laughed.

"Well, go dance with them."

Wren-at-Dawn grinned, "Yes, sir."

16 APPROVED BY A DOG

Morgan was seated between his grandchildren, who were bookended by their parents at either end of the row. In front of him, Debbie sat with the dog Owahah in her lap and her grandsons on one side of her and her daughter and son-in-law on the other side. When the service ended, Morgan asked both rows to join him for lunch.

"Oh, we've been invited to the Ranch for the afternoon," Becky frowned.

"Not a problem, that's where I was going to take you."

At the ranch, the children took off after dogs, as children will, and Becky and Debbie wandered with Morgan to the Jamaican Me Hungry Mess Hall.

Debbie spied Venutha and felt her concern loosen within her. She excused herself and went to speak with the teen.

"Hi, Venutha. How are you?"

The young woman-child glowed with happiness. "I'm fine. I'm terrific! How are you?"

"I'm better. I was wondering how your date went Friday night?

The girl paled. "Date?"

"Yes. With John Parker, the man from the bookstore. I couldn't help but overhear your plans."

Hreno and Jeremy came up beside her.

"It was fun. But it wasn't really a date. We're just friends."

"Who, John?" Hreno asked. "When do I get to meet this man? He's never at church."

"He has to work."

Jeremy chimed in, "Or so he says."

"Hey. You've met him. He was nice." Venutha was defensive.

"He had a nice car – red Chrysler Lebaron convertible. But he was old," Jeremy stated.

"Age doesn't matter."

"Yes," Debbie spoke firmly. "It does on this world. There are laws about age differences here."

"Hi, welcome to the Ranch. I'm Ben. My wife Joan is thrilled about crocheting. Thanks for teaching her."

Debbie shook the vet's hand, liking him immediately.

"I guess you know my children. Venutha, Hreno, and Jeremy."

Debbie looked confused.

Venutha supplied, "Daddy Ben adopted Hreno and me. Papa Pierre adopted Wren-at-Dawn and Jeremy. For the rest of the Horsemen and Dog Guards, Daddy Ben or Papa Pierre adopts them when the horses or dogs choose them."

"Oh."

"Listen, I wanted to introduce you to Pierre. Shall we go find him?"

Debbie smiled. "Just a minute. I'll be right with you."

Ben grinned and walked away.

"Venutha," Debbie turned so Ben couldn't read her lips. "None of my business, but you people seem to put a lot of stock into whether a person serves the light or the dark. Just, be careful around John Parker. Pray about it, or ask him flat out, 'whom do you serve?'"

"Wren-at-Dawn already did that." Venutha wouldn't meet Debbie's eyes.

"He didn't tell you, did he."

Jeremy replied, "No. He didn't. He said he didn't serve either one."

Owohah stopped beside Debbie and panted.

Venutha made hooting noises. The dog barked.

Jeremy made soft diphthongs and vowels sounds. The dog barked and panted.

Debbie's eyes felt like saucers. These children were actually communicating with Owohah. "What did he say?"

Jeremy looked at Venutha and shrugged. She spoke, "He says to listen to you and follow your advice. He says that you're going to be the friend of his master. That you will save his master from redemption and care for him as a grandmother."

"He said beta female."

"It's the same thing."

Jeremy rolled his eyes. "Anyway, Owohah said to listen to you."

"I've been approved by a dog."

Hreno smiled, "Welcome to the Ranch."

Pierre took Debbie's hand, listening to Ben's introduction.

She smiled, "We've met, haven't we? Years ago?"

"I've been here and there on this old world, and a few others, so maybe we have."

"Well, it is nice to meet you now. You're in charge of the horsemen, right?"

He held a hand beside his mouth and mock-whispered, "As long as they keep believing that, then I am."

She smiled and Morgan walked up beside her.

Pierre nodded at Morgan. "This place suits Ms. Debbie. Suits her real well."

Morgan took her elbow, "We're all hoping so."

He led her away.

"So what did you see?" Ben asked, not expecting Pierre to answer – he never did.

"Outside of the obvious world of pain and sorrow; more than she lets on but not more than she can handle. The rest is none of your business. But it might be Morgan's." Pierre chuckled.

Isabel Cortez stared at the photo attachments on her computer. "She's a little ugly, isn't she."

Jaro, her newest boy toy, glanced up from where he was kneeling beside her. "She looks sweet. Innocent."

Cortez tilted her head, examining the photos again. "I suppose so. I'd almost forgotten what innocence looks like."

She clicked reply and typed <<**Continue observation. Verify girl is Stelt's daughter.** >>

"It looks like she dances well," Jaro added. He pointed at one of the pictures. "Those men holding her elbows while Stelt is hitting the man at the table, who are they?"

"Refugees. People she lives with. This one with the beard," pointing to the older of the two, "is quite luscious, don't you think?"

17 UNCI

The boots on her feet were soft doe skin laced up her shins. They were comfortable and protected her along the miles and miles she had traveled. She wore a hooded cape of golden wool which crossed in front of her amply and was pinned with a bone and shell broach on her left shoulder. Her walking stick was from the branch of a sequoia she had gathered as a child and was worn smooth by years of her hand's caress. She walked quickly across the countryside, and as she walked, she prayed. Houses lined the darkened street, unoccupied or closely guarded from within. A man struggled to carry a woman – desiccated and stiff from being long dead – into his house. She strode past him, praying. An old woman came into her yard, across the street from where the traveler walked. "This is no place for your prayers!" the old woman shouted angrily.

Still the traveler prayed.

She didn't know where she was going. That wasn't important. Where wasn't important, just why. She was going because darkness had fallen and she needed to change the world back to the time of light.

She could hear children singing. The path she followed curved into a darkened field surrounded by rocks and caverns and stony paths. To her left along the path, along the journey, along the darkness in search of the light, she saw a mass of rubble – broken walls and timbers, a book flapping impotently in the wind, a pair of glasses, a child's shoe.

Her boots stopped walking; her staff stopped beating the rhythm of her steps. She sat by the rubble and listened to the song.

Many and great, O God, are Thy things,
Maker of earth and sky;
Thy hands have set the heavens with stars;
Thy fingers spread the mountains and plains.
Lo, at Thy Word the waters were formed;
Deep seas obey Thy voice.

Grant unto us communion with Thee,
Thou star abiding One;
Come unto us and dwell with us;
With Thee are found the gifts of life,
Bless us with life that has no end,
Eternal life with Thee.

As she listened, she pulled out the shawl she had been making and crocheted in rhythm with the children's song. This yarn was beautiful – soft gossamer fibers with strands of moonlight woven in. She made the shawl in a fillet pattern like an ancient net, soft yet incredibly strong. As she crocheted and the children sang, Earth shook and trembled and a darkness filled the mountainsides. Black beetles scurried out of a hole in the ground. The beetles heard the children singing and wanted to devour them. So the traveler-at-rest cast the shawl over the rubble, over the voices, hiding them from the hungry beetles. The glow of moonlight attracted a snowy owl from his journey across the nights' skin. He soared closer and spied the beetles. On silent wings he fell, gobbling the beetles and driving them back into their dark hole. The snowy owl was joined by other birds of prey and the beetles disappeared.

The traveler-at-rest smiled at the snowy owl, but he could not see her.

"Are you weaving, grandmother?" a rabbit spoke from beside her.

"Yes," she answered.

"It is so beautiful, may I touch it?" the rabbit asked.

"Yes," she answered.

"I hear it singing." The rabbit nestled into the soft shawl.

"The shawl does not sing. The children I have hidden safely under it sing."

The snowy owl landed beside her so the rabbit hid under the shawl, too.

The owl hooted plaintively, "I cannot see you, though I know you are there, my love."

Slowly, because she did not want to stop traveling and stay with the owl, she rolled up the shawl and placed it back inside her bag. The bunny clung to the shawl and was now nestled within the bag, safe from the beetles and the owl. But the children under the rubble cried out.

The owl's flock of other creatures quickly helped the children come up out of the rubble.

"I know you're there, my love," the owl hooted again.

But her moccasins began to move, across the plains, through the woods, over the mountains and under the caverns. At night, she could not hear the owl, but she could see him soaring high above her.

The rabbit remained safe within Grandmother Spider's weaving bag.

Debbie opened her eyes. She lay there, breathing like she'd been running. Sleep disturbances caused by grief, that's what these dreams must be. She felt she wasn't really in mourning for her late husband. The emotion, had she been honest with herself, was more along the lines of relief. But once, long ago, when she had truly suffered grief, followed so quickly in child years by the *horrible thing*, she had had similar dreams. Lucid dreams, that's what Rosa's mother called them. She began having the dreams again, every once and a while, five years ago. But since she'd moved here to Morning Creek, they seemed to haunt her every other night.

She took a steadying breath and rolled out of bed. The clock read two fifteen. Quietly, she turned on the lamp and picked up her crochet bag. She was making a shawl for a friend: pearlized white cotton fillet with an f hook and a rabbit motif. Debbie sat in the arm chair and began to crochet. She finished one row and turned the shawl. Bright red covered nine inches along the edge. Debbie frowned and pulled it to her face for a closer look. It looked like red clay dust; the kind she remembered from her childhood. Her father had been a missionary to the Lakota tribes in South Dakota, and the soil there was red clay, like the people's skin. The Lakota tell the story of the Great Flood, where the blood of everyone who drowned became the rocks in the pipestone quarry. Red stones, red clay; it was a beautiful land.

Debbie closed her eyes, remembering the dream. She shook her head and continued to crochet.

The prayer shawl group had grown to include several girls from the Ranch and their dogs and horses. Debbie made the dogs and horses stay outside, at least, that was the plan, but Owohah was allowed to stay because he slept at her feet, and Hreno's cairn terrier was teaching Baby Ben to walk. The others darted inside any time the door was opened and then chased out again.

Their meeting had come to a close and everyone was walking outside when a Nissan Forrester pulled into the drive across the way and Morgan got out.

Debbie felt her cheeks blush and her heart raced.

Morgan went around the car and opened the door. Even across the cemetery, the women could hear the excited chatter of a boy.

"Looks like Morgan has company," Bea said.

The dogs began to growl. Hackles rose as the pack turned and sniffed the air.

The child came out of the passenger seat, talking ninety-miles-a-minute while Morgan got a duffle bag out of the back.

Owohah crouched and then sprang forward, barking defensively. The boy looked up in shock. The dogs headed straight at him. Morgan shouted something and the boy ran. He took off into the cemetery, bounding over gravestones and bouncing off of marble slabs. He made a hooting sound with every other step.

The Dog Guards yelled commands at their dogs, but the canines ignored them and zigzagged through the cemetery after the boy.

The boy circled around, drawing the dogs further away, and then he doubled back. He saw the women gathered and began to yell, "Unci, unci! Hide me!"

It had been forty years since Debbie had last heard the Lakota language, but she remembered it immediately. She shouted in the ancient tongue, "Here, run here!"

She yanked out the white shawl she'd just finished and flapped it in the air, to let him find her. He ran to her with dogs close behind. Debbie began running to him and they met at the edge of the parking lot. He flung his arms around her and she wrapped him in the shawl.

The Dog Guards stepped between their dogs and Debbie, yelling.

Morgan joined them at a full run.

"They are going to eat me, Unci!" the boy panted in Lakota, clinging to Debbie.

"I won't let them eat you, Rabbit," she soothed him.

"They smell the darkness on you, that's all," Hreno was at his side. She lifted one edge of the encompassing shawl and grinned at the boy. "You're like me. You're a weave. Once you've lost the stench of despair, the dogs will love you."

"No, no, they'll eat me. Keep me safe from the monsters, Unci. Keep me safe like you did the singing children under the stones."

Debbie kissed the top of his head, "I promise. I won't let them hurt you."

"Are you sure that's why the dogs attacked him?" Gwen asked.

Hreno nodded. "Can't you smell him?"

"I don't smell. Uncle Owl made me shower this morning." He looked up at Debbie. "I don't smell, do I, Unci?"

"I think," she smiled, enjoying the sound of Lakota again. "You smell like a bunny rabbit. And Owohah loves to chase bunnies. When you started running, he thought you were playing a running game. Isn't that right, Owoha?"

The dog in question snorted and sat down.

"Does the beast understand you, Grandmother?"

"Do you understand the boy, Debbie?" Morgan asked.

"Yes," to both of them, but she said it in Lakota.

"I think," Gwen stepped forward, "it is lunchtime. All Dog Guard and Horsemen should go to the Ranch. The rest of you should go home or to the Refuge. And Debbie, Morgan, and your new friend should come with me to Atticus' office."

"I'll just stay here," came the voice from under the shawl.

"Hreno, can you take Owoha home with you?" Debbie asked.

"I'll try, but he pretty much doesn't listen to anybody."

"Yes. Go away. Take the beast away. He wants to eat me. I know he does. Grandmother will keep me safe under her shawl, but you take the Owoha away."

"What language is he speaking?" Bea spoke softly.

"This is the weave you rescued?" Gwen asked.

Morgan nodded.

Owoha remained near Debbie, ignoring Hreno completely.

Morgan squatted beside the boy and patted his elbow. "They're not going to hurt you. They guard us against the darkness. You understand me?"

The boy nodded, but did not relinquish his grip around Debbie.

"Whom do you serve?" Gwen demanded.

"The light. I serve the light."

Debbie rubbed his back. "He said he serves the light."

Morgan spoke to Gwen, "You let Debbie through a portal?"

"She refuses to pray with Atticus. Of course we haven't let her through."

"So he's speaking a language she can understand. An Earth language?"

"It must be. Unless she's not who she claims to be."

Debbie bristled, "*She* is standing right here."

"That beast is still there. He still wants to gobble me up. You won't let him, right, Grandmother?"

"I promise, Rabbit. You're safe."

"Safe under your shawl."

"Yes. Now, you'll have to let go of me a little."

"Can I stay under the shawl?"

"Yes."

The boy kept the shawl wrapped over his head and shoulders. He turned and did a little jig as he spoke to Awohah, "You can't get me, Awohah. I am under Grandmother's protective shawl and you can't hurt me!"

Awoha huffed out a dog laugh, stood, and padded away.

"How is it that you can understand him?"

"Morgan, let's hold all questions until we get to Atticus' office. I'll meet you there after I drop the children with Visolela."

Morgan nodded and glanced sideways at Debbie.

"I feel like I've been called into the principal's office."

He smiled at her remark. "Come on, boy. Let's get back in the car."

103

"Oh, the car! I like the car. It goes fast. Zoom! Very fast. Not like the plane. It was so fast I threw up. But the car goes fast, too. And it has songs. 'Everybody wants to go to heaven!' Like that. Happy songs. And it has soft chairs, but I don't like the seat belt. With Grandmother's shawl around me, I'll be safe so I don't need the seat belt."

"Yes, you do," Morgan stated.

"You speak Lakota?"

"What?"

"The boy, he's speaking Lakota and you understand him. You just answered him in Lakota."

Morgan opened the passenger door, held the boy back, and offered Debbie the seat. He then opened the back door and the boy crawled in.

"This is nice! It's like a bed that moves. I like the smell too, and it has little drawers and pockets." The boy opened and shut every compartment and the windows, too.

Morgan started the car. "Seat belt."

"But I have the shawl."

"Bunny, put on your seat belt," Debbie spoke firmly.

"Yes, Unci."

"Why does he call you *unci*?"

"I thought you spoke Lakota."

Morgan sighed. "You've been here a while now. Ever notice how everyone seems to speak the same language?"

"Only those who have been through a portal. And not everyone speaks the same language. I think everyone comprehends whatever language is spoken, like you all had babel fish stuck in your ears, or you've all been in the TARDIS. A universal translator."

Morgan blinked, "You watch Dr. Who?"

Debbie smirked, "I have many talents."

Morgan blushed.

It seemed so incongruous, this secret agent colonel blushing at an innocent remark. Debbie forged ahead, "So, you understand Bunny but you don't speak Lakota."

"That's part of it," Morgan flashed his badge at the security guard at the gate. The badge was a formality which allowed the cameras time to take pictures of the car's occupants.

"Where are we going, Owl?" He slung his arms over the back of the seat. "What is this place? It's big. And look at all the children. Is this a livestock pavilion, too? You told me you serve the light, Snowy Owl. Why would you keep children in a livestock pavilion?"

"Put your seat belt back on," Debbie scolded.

"But I can't see everything from back here."

"Open the windows." Morgan suggested. "After you put on the seat belt."

"But it's hot outside." They heard a click. "If I open the windows, summer rushes in."

Morgan drew a deep breath again.

"Wow! Look at the weave on that building!"

"Turn around, sit down, and put your seat belt on!" Morgan growled.

"It is on." The boy twisted under its constraints to face forward. "This world sure has a lot of rules. Why would they put a door on a plane if you can't open it? And why can't you pee when you need to pee?"

Morgan put a trembling hand to his right eyebrow.

"Talkative little bugger," Debbie grinned.

"He talks constantly. The last day and a half have lasted a century."

"Hey, why did you stop? Can I get out now? Can I take off the seat belt?"

"Stay put. I'll come around and get you."

"Why? Is it dangerous? Are there beasts here?" The boy pulled the shawl over his head.

Morgan opened Debbie's door and then the boy's. "This is the safest place on my planet."

He jumped out and took Debbie's hand, "Because you've hidden this place under our shawl, right Unci?"

"No. It's safe because no one knows it's here."

"It's more than that," Morgan started, but didn't complete the thought.

Atticus met them inside the narthex. He nodded at Debbie, embraced Morgan and then knelt in front of the boy, who pulled the shawl over his head and face again.

"My name is Atticus. I am a Minister of God. I welcome you here to the Refuge. Let's go talk together in my office. You'll like the elevator, Weave."

The boy lifted the shawl just enough to look at Debbie.

She smiled and nodded. He pulled the shawl down to his shoulders and took her hand again.

"Let's take the stairs."

Atticus blinked at Morgan.

"Uncle Owl taught me all about elevators, Atticus of God. There were so many buttons: one, two, three, four, five, six, eight, nineteen, twenty-two, forty-seven, thirty-five, twelve."

"The stairs it is," the preacher grinned.

Once Atticus closed the door, Morgan took the armchair and Debbie and the boy sat on the coach.

"This is just like Uncle Owl's car. But I don't see the buttons to play music. I like music. 'Hillbilly bone ba-bone, ba-bone-bone!'"

Atticus glowered, "Morgan, just when I think I can trust you whole-heartedly, I find out this – that you're a country music fan. I'm shocked and dismayed."

"Well, 'some beach'."

Debbie shook her head and smiled.

The door opened and Gwen walked in. She took the other chair after kissing her husband.

"Weave. You know my name is Atticus, and Morgan found you. This is Debbie, and my wife is Gwen. What's your name?"

"I am Weave of Altrail." He stood and bowed. "But I don't want to be Weave of Altrail anymore. Uncle Owl said I don't have to be. I wasn't sure I wanted to come with him because, sometimes, even the nicest person lies. And sometimes people lie so well you don't know it's a lie. But then I saw Unci was here, too. So I'd like to stay here and be Weave of Unci. Or Weave of Owl, if he is the Strategia Luce. I could even be Weave of Atticus, if you'll let me stay near Uncle Owl and Grandmother Debbie."

"We'll look into that. But first, I need you to answer some questions."

The weave sat beside Debbie. She was nervous, so she took out her hook and one end of a skein of Redheart Peruvian yarn and began to crochet.

"I have to tell you, Debbie, I'm not comfortable with you being here. You're new to us, and you have yet to meet with me to pray."

She raised an eyebrow but said nothing. The multicolored yarn shifted from copper to turquoise. Beside her, the weave's eyes widened.

"But Morgan has mentioned several incidents to me which seem to suggest you are – or could be – one of us. And this child knows you, even though he just set foot on this planet two days ago and told Morgan he'd never been here before. Mitchell has found no evidence that you've ever been through a portal. So that leaves one realm where you and the child could have met. And that also supports Morgan's assumption that you're a dreamwalker."

Debbie's hands stilled. She looked at Morgan, at Gwen, at Atticus, and gauged the distance to the door. "You have me at a disadvantage. I would really like to be as far away from this crazy little town as I could get. But my daughter lives here. Her family lives here. I have nowhere else to go. No money, no transportation. No home other than what my son-in-law can provide for me. So I can't just stand up and walk away from this office, because I don't know the ramifications of such an action." She picked up the yarn and hook again. "But I'm not a dreamwalker."

"Weave, how do you know Debbie?" Morgan asked.

"Oh, she kept me safe, when I ran away after the soldiers began to be killed."

"Did she find you?"

"No, I found her. First, I heard the children singing, 'Wa-kantanka taku nitawa. ' So I ran toward them, but the ground was covered by a white web that glowed with goodness. It was being woven by Unci."

"Debbie?"

"Yes, Grandmother Debbie. She was weaving it and had cast it over the children underground so the dark soldiers could not find them."

Debbie's face clouded with the remnant of a dream from two nights before.

"And then what happened?" Atticus asked.

"And then a huge snow white owl flew over me and I was afraid but Grandmother let me hide under the shawl with the children. I didn't know he was a good man. Not then. Not until Grandmother told me to go with him. 'It's alright, little bunny,' she told me. 'Go with the General and he will keep you safe. ' So I stayed with Uncle Owl and he took me aboard a plane and then rode in a car and he brought me right back to Grandmother. And see – this is the shawl she covered the children with!" He held it up.

"Does any of this sound familiar?" Morgan glared at her.

"What he means by 'children underground.'" She side-stepped Morgan's question.

"There was an earthquake Friday in South Dakota. A school full of orphaned children collapsed, but it was in such a remote part of the Black Hills, no one knew to get help."

"I haven't been in South Dakota since I was a child."

"You speak Lakota," Gwen remarked.

"My father was a missionary in that area," she offered, and continued her hand-craft.

"You're making the snow now, Grandmother," Bunny whispered. "See?" he traced the colored stitches. "Turquoise of water, brown of earth, white of snow. You're weaving a mountain, aren't you, Grandmother."

"The children in the orphanage," Debbie side-stepped again. "Are they alright?"

"Yes!" Bunny offered. "There was blood and guts and puke and poop everywhere, but Snowy Owl's soldiers dug up the rocks and the children all came out."

Debbie smiled without looking up. "And the – dark soldiers? What became of them?

Gwen snapped, "That's classified."

Bunny peeked around to look at Gwen and then pushed himself under Debbie's arm. "Is it going to be a very large mountain?"

Debbie shook her head. "Just a bunny-sized mountain, to wear on your head, so that you won't have bad dreams."

"So my redeemer can't find me?"

Debbie glanced at the stoic faces of Morgan and Atticus. Gwen rubbed her hands over her abdomen.

"I don't want her to find me, Grandmother. She sharpens the knife of redemption all the time, to slay me rather than allow me to turn to despair."

Morgan wouldn't meet her eyes.

Debbie spoke softly, trying to cover her anger, "Can she find you here?"

The boy nodded and covered his face with the shawl. "We are woven together. She can follow the threads between us, no matter what world, as long as she lives."

He spoke slowly, "But I don't want her to die. She's my mommy."

Debbie was gasping for breath. Her fingers flew as they formed the cap. Her scarred left shoulder ached and twinged.

"Why does he speak Lakota? I thought we bound our languages with the first sentient being on each world," Morgan asked.

"The strongest souls," Gwen corrected. "That's why Otka can speak with dragons and Venutha to dogs and horses."

"You are very strong soul, Uncle Owl, but the children singing through the web bound my tongue."

"I don't get it," Atticus sighed.

"The children were singing a hymn by Joseph Renville from the Dakota Indian Hymnal. My father ended every funeral with it." Debbie began to sing, "Wakantanka taku nitawa."

"Maker of Earth and Sky," Bunny continued the song. "Thy hands have set the heavens with stars; Thy fingers spread the mountains and plains." His voice drifted off and he pressed himself against Debbie's arm.

Gwen perched forward, "Now, how did you know that?"

"The same way the weave knew to call me General; because Debbie told him to. I just received notification this morning that I've been nominated for the rank. But Debbie wrote me a note a month ago, when she gave me a cap. 'Congratulations, General.'"

Debbie's hands stilled. She thought very carefully about what she was going to say. But, this little boy had a killer tied to him metaphysically, and it was obvious this cult had no idea how to help him. Taking a calming breath, she began, "You all act like this whole scenario is something new and unique to Earth. This war – light against dark, hope against despair – it's been going on for millennium. You don't have a monopoly on ESP, or dreamwalking, or spiritual healing, or the space-time continuum. The Native American came to this planet through a portal – it's in all of their legends. You're children. No, you're adolescents who have discovered what naked flesh feels like. And like adolescents, you believe no one else in all creation could be experiencing what you are going through.

"You're fools. You hide yourself on this compound – you even removed the town of Morning Creek from Mapquest and Rand-McNally – I checked! Goggle-Earth goes all gray and wispy when I loaded the coordinates. How you accomplished that is a technological conspiracy! You think you're the only ones given God's blessing to know about this war. You squelch CNN and Fox News; you censor the internet. You're so busy hoarding your secrets; you've forgotten to ask questions. Questions that are so obvious someone must be blocking your brains to keep you from seeing them!"

"Like what?" Atticus asked.

"Like – how can you breathe on another world? How can you eat the native foods and understand the language?"

"The portal," Gwen began.

"Exactly," Debbie snarled. "The portal. It changes your mind; it changes your body. And you are so excited to be able to see the sunsets of alien planets; you neglect to ask – what else did the portal change? And more to the point – why?"

The three adults answered in unison, "To hold back the dark."

Debbie gaped. "See? That didn't come from three individual people. That answer came from one omnipotent sentience."

Once again, Debbie observed the three adults do a slow blink, as if they were just about to sneeze.

Atticus sniffed and grinned, "So Morgan, how long have you been a country music fan?"

"Ever since I learned that girls love to two-step."

Debbie felt the rage building within her. She stood. "Somebody's coming to kill this child, unless Gwen's definition of *classified* means you stood them all against a wall and shot them. And Hreno is at risk, too. She says her father's in prison. Are you sure? She's been having horrible nightmares. But you people – you didn't even ask why."

Morgan stood and reached out for her.

"Just leave me alone, General." Debbie held up her fists.

"Don't yell. Don't yell at Uncle Owl. He loves you; I heard him say so when you were in the dream world." Bunny pushed his way between them and held onto Debbie's elbows.

She moved her fists to her mouth. Bunny mimicked her, covering his mouth, too. "Yes," he whispered. "No more shouting. The darkness can hear you when you're angry."

"Look," Morgan drew a deep breath and glanced at Atticus, who nodded reluctantly. "You're right, things aren't always as they seem. But no matter your opinion of the situation, know that one of our main goals here is to keep children safe. Especially children like Bunny and Hreno. You have to trust us."

Debbie took a step backward.

"She's not going to." Gwen turned to her husband. "Pierre said that every person she has ever trusted in her life betrayed her in some way."

Morgan corrected, "Not everyone. She trusts herself. She trusts her own instincts and her faith." He put his hand on the boy's head, "Bunny trusts her, don't you, son?"

He nodded vigorously, "She serves the light."

Atticus calmly observed Debbie.

"Would you take Bunny down into the sanctuary and wait for me? I have something to discuss with Atticus. Then I'll take you home. Or, I'll take you to the airport with enough money to go wherever you want to go."

"The airport?" Bunny took Debbie's hand. "You don't want to go there, Grandmother. They go too fast and take you far away. I don't want you to go far away."

"I'll take him into the sanctuary. But I won't pray with you, Atticus."

"OK," the preacher said.

She glared at Morgan before exiting with Bunny.

"Are you sure about her?"

Atticus answered Morgan immediately, "Absolutely."

"You don't think her grief will overwhelm her?" Gwen sat back down.

"I just think we should tell her."

"Yeah, because being up front and honest worked so well with you."

The two men laughed, remembering.

"So you had the soldiers placed into the penn? Including the weave's redeemer?"

"Yes, Cortez has it all under control. She's training them as if they were still soldiers. It keeps the suicides and murders down and gives them something familiar to do."

"Do you think Debbie's right about Hreno?" Gwen rubbed her tummy.

"I'll give Ben a call. We might want to transfer her to Mitchell's dorm for a week or two. Call it intensive training. By then, the waystation should be ready, and we've already made arrangements for heavy guards there." Atticus came around the desk. "Now, what else?"

"CNN wants an exclusive."

Atticus glanced at Gwen. She frowned, "Again?"

"It's Sophia Sage. Again. She says she'll hold the lid on everything for five years, and then she'll publish, but she wants to come visit, do a full coverage. And she wants to go to another world as part of it."

"Absolutely not!" Gwen shouted.

Atticus held up a finger. "The darkness can hear you when you shout."

"It's going to come out eventually. A little bit here, a lot there. We have to constantly monitor the web to censor out any mention of us. But one day, dark soldiers are going to attack someplace where we can't squelch it. This way, we control what, how much, and when."

"Is she willing to pray with me?'

"For what it's worth – yes."

"Can't we just feed her a little bit?" Gwen asked.

"Absolutely." Morgan perched. "I choose who she interviews, who she meets, what she sees. I can keep her out of the compound for at least a year, setting up visits with eye-witnesses and autopsy reports."

"Could she help squelch other networks' reports?"

"Yes, I believe so. I could make that part of the deal." Morgan's mouth twisted in wry humor. "If nothing else, we could send her into a portal of light and if she is not willing to serve the light, problem solved."

Atticus grimaced and placed his hand on his side. The hairs on Morgan's arms and legs tingled. Gwen bent her head, wincing.

The preacher took a deep breath, "Mitchell's getting stronger. He's a wilder; that's what the Icsona call him. They think he'll flash into a portal and disappear if we can't get him stabilized."

Gwen went to her husband's side. "The more weaves we gather, the more information we'll have. Eventually, we'll find someone who can deal with this."

Atticus tilted his head back and gaped in silent agony.

Debbie took Bunny into the elevator with the admonition that he punch one and only one button. As the door opened onto the narthex, she felt a stabbing pain in her shoulder and the hairs along her arms tingled. Bunny took her hand and pressed against her.

They walked out of the elevator and went to the double doors leading into the sanctuary. When activated, bolts would lock the doors in place, as a blast door should the need arise. But Debbie didn't know this. She knew that beyond these doors, something was happening that drew her heart forward just as her mind was trying to retreat.

Inside the sanctuary, the light was too brilliant to see anything but vague shapes. Bunny held the shawl over his eyes with one hand. "Angels," he whispered. "Bringers of Light."

Debbie paused at the edge of a pew and let her eyes adjust.

"Do you see them, Grandmother? Do you see the angels?"

Debbie saw a globe of light encompassing the altar area below the pulpit and in front of the pews. Something moved within the globe – something massive and pure white. Debbie held her breath and the figure resolved itself. Horns, like ancient tree branches curved over white curls of fur. A massive muzzle and nostrils with dark black eyes nine feet above the ground. The shoulders were like marble, pure white and solid as stone. The body was massive yet muscular. Four trunks as legs ended with black hooves larger than cornerstones. In Debbie's mind, she could hear them thundering across a plain. The words tumbled out as a name, "The White Buffalo."

From out of the Buffalo's shoulder stepped a maiden. The most beautiful woman-child Debbie had ever seen. The Calf-Maiden smiled at her and opened her mouth, speaking words which Debbie could not hear.

The White Cloud. The White Buffalo. The Calf-Maiden. They formed a trinity, just as her father had taught her. God was the White Cloud. Jesus was the Buffalo. The Spirit was the Maiden.

She felt her arm being tugged and followed it. Bunny led her to the front of the church. Her skin felt like it was going to crawl off.

Bunny whispered, "It's a beautiful weave. There are so many strands. I can only follow a few of them. Can you teach me this?"

The Calf-Maiden answered in a voice of crystal thunder, "He doesn't know what he's weaving. He is just opening himself up to God."

"Are the prophecies fulfilled?" Debbie asked.

"Prophecies?"

Debbie reached out a hand and dared to stroke the fetlocks of the White Buffalo. It felt like raw wool, before it is combed, before it is spun. Raw and wild and she knew that a blanket woven from his fur would keep a body from freezing to death. She knew that a shawl made from this wool would keep out the glacier winds. Baby booties made from this wool would protect the child no matter where it roamed. She curled her fingers into a swatch of this magnificent fur and pulled. It gave but a little. She yanked it.

The light disappeared and the sanctuary was dark in its absence.

"Ow! What did you do that for?" an adolescent voice whined.

Debbie blinked, her eyes slowly adjusting to normal daylight. Before her stood a young man, no more than sixteen, and the blind girl with the burned skin. The boy was holding his forehead.

Debbie looked at the curls of black hair still clutched between her fingers. She'd yanked them out of the White Buffalo, but it was the boy before her who was missing a handful of hair.

The girl stepped away from the boy. "I sense two weaves. Who are you?"

"I am Weave of Owl and Atticus and Grandmother," Bunny supplied. "And this is Grandmother Debbie."

"I am Shadow, and this is Mitchell."

The youth frowned but said, "Hello."

Upstairs, Morgan shivered as he felt the portal close. "What did you mean when you said Debbie wouldn't trust us?"

Gwen kept her eyes on her husband's ashen face. Still, after all these years, the wound could kill him. "Pierre saw something when he met her. Something huge. You know he never reveals what he sees, but he drew me aside and told me that her journey here has taken more than three dozen years and that she will never trust us because of her mother."

"What about her mother?" Atticus asked Morgan.

The colonel frowned. "She's alive and well and living in a nursing home in Plant City, Florida. She was a Salvation Army Major."

"Was the Major or her husband the Lakota Missionary Debbie mentioned?" Atticus wiped his face and drew a deep, pain-free breath.

"She has been a widow for at least thirty years. Gabriel mentioned that the husband might have been killed the last year of Viet Nam, but he wasn't sure. They're not close. When Becky was having medical problems with her pregnancy, Debbie's mother refused to provide medical records. Gabriel was understandably upset. I do know that Debbie changed her last name to Smith when she turned sixteen. I don't know about her before then."

Gwen snorted.

"With the earthquakes and missing children, I did a basic background check on Debbie. Gabriel vouched for her."

"How far did you go back?" the warrior asked.

"Thirty years. From when she legally changed her name."

Atticus glanced at his wife, "Three dozen equals thirty-six, last time I counted."

Morgan frowned. He'd missed it, this secret hidden behind Debbie. "There is no record of Debbie before her sixteenth birthday."

Atticus held his hand up and pointed out the window. "I have three thousand children without a paper trail."

Morgan stood, "I'll find out."

18 NOT HER BLOOD

"Momma," The cold wind stole the syllables from her mouth. She ran along the path that wove through the trees. "Momma!"

A raven cried out from the boughs and for a brief moment, Debbie was sure it was laughing at her.

"Momma!" she sobbed, but the winds scoured those tears from her cheeks. Night was falling and she was alone and her mother had left her. She'd left her here, in the woods, cold and frightened. Abandoned.

"Momma!"

Debbie awoke, gasping for breath. She hadn't had that dream in decades. Why now? She hadn't been able to sleep Monday night. She looked at the clock – 2:15 Wednesday morning. She got up and went down to the kitchen. Her shoulder ached, as it did every now and then. Tonight, it itched, too. She hardly ever looked at it anymore – the scar between her shoulder and collar bone; just inches from her heart. Tonight, her fingertips lingered on the scar, remembering the sorrow, the anger, the terror. Hearing Lakota again, speaking it again, after three dozen years; Debbie shuddered and shut out the memories. She'd even changed her name to blot her parents – her father – from her life.

She used to pray for the White Buffalo and Calf-Maiden to bring her mother back. Five years with a psychologist had convinced her that her vision had been just a figment of her imagination, brought on by the trauma that was evidenced by the scar. But Monday, she saw the White Buffalo. She spoke with the Calf-Maiden. She recognized the blinding light through which her mother had stepped.

The coffee mug in her hands slipped and shattered on the tile floor as realization stabbed into her like the knife had so many years earlier – her father had not murdered her mother. Her mother had walked into a portal of light.

The kitchen folded in and around her and she collapsed as the phone began to ring.

After hanging up from Gabriel, Morgan called the clinic. Chi would be right there. Bunny stood ready at the door, sleepy and wrapped in Debbie's white shawl, but anxious for them to get to Debbie.

Morgan kept going over Gabriel's words, "There's blood everywhere!" He opened the door and Bunny ran to the car.

The lights were on all over Gabriel's house. Becky met him at the door, "She's in the living room. Gabriel's trying to stop the bleeding."

The phone rang and Thomas picked it up. "Yeah Aunt Missy, Grandpa Morgan's here. Doctor Chi's coming."

Morgan took the phone, "Hey Sweetie. I'm sending Thomas and Devin over to stay with you. And Bunny, too. And Missy, bring a bottle of whiskey. See you soon."

He patted Thomas's head. "Get your little brother's and your sleeping bags and a blanket for Bunny. Aunt Missy's going to come over and take you next door. You're going to spend the night with her."

"But Grandma Debbie," the boy began.

"She'll be alright. Now, hop to it. Aunt Missy will be right here."

"Is that OK, Mom?"

Becky nodded.

Bunny crept toward the room with the bright light while Morgan was on the phone. He could see the silhouette of Grandma Debbie on the couch and a man leaning over her. Debbie glowed. Bunny crept closer. Blood bubbled between the man's fingers.

"Damn it, it won't stop! I can't stop the bleeding."

Morgan grabbed the boy's shoulder. "Go wait for my daughter in the hallway."

"Morgan, bring me another towel. This one's soaked through."

Morgan dashed out of the room. Bunny walked to the couch and looked down at Grandma Debbie's faced. She was so bright, Bunny had to squint.

"Morgan, the towel!" Gabriel shouted.

"It's not her blood," Bunny told him. The little boy placed his hands on her cheeks and gently kissed her forehead. He felt the power surge into him. It was too much, too great. He was afraid. He reached out and took Morgan's arm. The power poured into the old soldier.

Morgan gasped as Bunny took his arm. Gabriel snatched at the towel, their fingers touched and the power flowed through the connection.

Bunny nodded; he was too filled with the light to speak.

"Becky, come here!" Gabriel commanded.

She dashed in, followed by Missy and the boys.

"Take my hand. Quickly! Boys, join hands. That's it. Can you feel it?"

Chi walked in and gently pushed Gabriel aside. He pulled back Debbie's blood-soaked gown and examined the scar tissue beneath. He used the fresh towel to blot at the blood still seeping up through the unbroken skin.

The doctor glanced at the little boy, pressing his cheek against Debbie's brow. He traced the scar and spoke softly. "You know what this is?"

Bunny nodded.

"You've seen it before?"

He nodded again.

"You drew the power away."

Bunny nodded and closed his eyes. His tears moistened her forehead.

"Debbie, can you hear me?" Chi took her pulse.

"Wake up, Grandmother." Bunny kissed her forehead again. "Please wake up."

The light dimmed, surged, and dimmed again. Moaning filled the room.

"Please wake up, Grandmother. I need you. And Uncle Owl loves you. Don't turn. Don't lose yourself. We saw the dream, both Uncle Owl and me. You lost your momma. I lost my momma, too. But I found you. Don't turn to despair. Please wake up."

The moaning stopped, replaced by sobbing. The light blinked out; the power with it.

"Good work, son." Chi touched Bunny's shoulder. "You saved her."

Debbie's eyes fluttered open. "What? Why are you? Where am I?"

Morgan dropped to one knee and hugged Bunny.

Chi helped her sit up. "We're taking you to the clinic. You're going to rest there for a few days. Can you remember what happened?"

Debbie swayed on the coach as Becky drew a blanket over her shoulders.

She couldn't speak, but the thought sank into her heart: *He didn't kill her. My father didn't kill my mother.* She buried her face in her hands and cried.

19 GIRLY GIRL

Gabriel's cell phone vibrated during the anthem and he checked the number. He punched the code for the text WAIT. Kissing his wife, he headed out of the sanctuary. Normally, all cell phones were blocked inside the church building, except those reprogrammed by Tyler, like Gabriel's and Morgan's.

Once outside, Gabriel spoke. "What's up?"

"Sheriff, I just got a call from a fisherman says he found a body down by Black Creek. Says it looks real bad."

"Black Creek?"

His receptionist filled him in, "About ten miles south of Morning Creek, follow the highway and there's a turn off to a picnic area. Picnic area was built there as a memorial at end of the second world war, but no one goes there anymore. You can't miss it."

Gabriel sighed; he'd missed a few locations that the locals took for granted. But he remembered something about Black Creek and had seen it on the map. "Call Eric and have him meet me there."

He got in his cruiser and began texting Morgan: CALLED 2 DOA @ BLACK CREEK. PLZ DRIVE FAM HOME. Gabriel turned on the siren only after he'd cleared the compound.

The county coroner Eric Rodriguez met him there. "Eric," Gabriel nodded.

"Sorry you had to be called away from church, Sheriff. I myself was in the middle of a luscious dream. She was a redhead this time." Eric was five foot five, two-hundred-sixty pounds, balding with a shiny face and a vivid imagination. "You'll want to rope off the area."

"You already looked at the scene?" Displeased with Eric, again.

"Yep. It's bad."

Gabriel stopped. "So?"

"Caucasian female. Approximately thirty-five, forty years old. Naked except for, well, you'll see. I'll put the death no less than three, no more than five days. Not officially though, because, by the look of her, it took her quite a while to die."

They headed down a worn path toward the creek. Gabriel's skin began to crawl. "This is a place of darkness."

"Yeah, it has history." Eric spoke over his shoulder, "In the seventeen hundreds, the landing used to be run by a ferry boat with a nice little trading post on that side, over there. Story has it; the ferry boat captain might take a dislike to someone and would slaughter them, tossing their bodies into the creek half-way across. He'd keep the things in their luggage and sell them in the trading post."

"So what happened to the trading post?"

"Well, the other story, it sort of lends itself to the first story, says a local Creek chief by the name of Black massacred the trading post and burnt it to the ground to avenge his daughter's murder -- seems she didn't quite make it all the way across the creek. So, Black Creek could mean bad creek or Black Indian. See?"

Gabriel grunted, watching the terrain more than listening to Eric.

"Used to hang run-away slaves and other criminals from the trees, just let their bodies decompose into the creek during the 1800's. Between the wars – the world wars – a school teacher thought she'd teach her students to swim the hard way – tossed them in clothes and all. Seven of them never learned to swim.

Townfolk built the picnic area to commemorate it, sort of as a memorial-slash-fun-for-the-kiddies idea. And see that bridge down the way? Thirty years ago, some high school kid drove his truck off the bridge, only he had the whole football team in the back."

The path curved and dropped sharply.

"And then there's the mess about your preacher."

Gabriel stopped. "What about him?"

"Oh, that's right, you weren't here then. Well, it was my first year here out of the service."

"Long story short, OK Eric?"

"Whatever. Your preacher's first wife sacrificed their little boy on that there barbecue pit and then slit her own wrists."

"That BBQ pit there with the body on it now?"

"That's the one." Eric stopped, careful not to contaminate the area with his foot prints.

At one time, she must have been a beautiful woman.

"The coals were still smoldering when the fisherman found her. She's been tortured but most likely not raped while she was alive and after she'd died. Note the knitted hat."

"It's a crocheted cap." Gabriel felt nauseous.

"Yeah? Well, it most likely belonged to the killer and was used as a marker. Some leave things; others take things. This wasn't the first time he's killed someone."

"Serial killer?"

"It'd be my guess."

Gabriel nodded, trying to distance himself from the familiarity of his mother-in-law's bright pink cap displayed on the victim's head.

Morgan drove Gabriel's family back to the church that evening after everyone had spent another pleasant day at the Ranch. As they entered the sanctuary, Gabriel arrived. He waved at Morgan and then at Tyler; they both stepped aside to speak with him.

Gabriel kept his voice low. "We'll need to discuss this with Atticus as soon as possible. And warn the citizens."

"You're sure the cap belonged to Debbie?" Morgan asked. He glanced through the double doors into the sanctuary. Debbie had one arm around Venutha and the other around Hreno. She looked rested and happy. "There must be a dozen women here now who crochet. And thousands of women around the state who crochet."

Gabriel sighed, "I remember the yarn color. It's called Girly Girl. A week ago Saturday, she asked me to drop her off at the fabric store when Becky and I went grocery shopping. I gave her twenty dollars, because I know she usually buys three skeins of whatever color she gets. She made the first cap on the way home in the car, and I joked about her being *tickled pink* with the yarn. She told me then, it's called Girly Girl. She was really excited because the store had just gotten it in. She was upset when we didn't let her take it to the clinic. Look," he pointed. "You can see it sticking out of her bag."

Tyler moderated, "From what Ricean tells me, the women make the caps to give them away. Maybe Debbie gave the victim a cap."

"One way to find out," Morgan led the other men into the sanctuary.

"Debbie, the three of us were just wondering – how many caps can you make from a hotdog of yarn?"

She laughed at Morgan, "A hotdog? You mean, a skein? Well, it depends on the weight of the yarn and size of the hook."

"How about that pretty pink yarn you've got in your bag. What about that one?"

"This?" She pulled it out. "It's four-ply by Redheart. Good, durable, consistent. I can make six adult-sized caps from a full five ounce skein."

"How many have you made?"

"Funny you should ask. I've made four, but I seemed to have lost one. And my scissors are missing, too."

Tyler picked up the lead, "It's a pretty color. I bet my wife would like it. What's it called?"

"This is Girly Girl."

Beside her, Hreno let out a little shriek.

"What?" Morgan asked.

Hreno paled. "My father used to call me that: Girly girl."

Debbie shoved the yarn back inside the bag. "Well, sometimes fathers," Debbie caught her breathe and bit her lip. "Never mind."

Gabriel took the straps of the bag. "I need to have this, Mom. I'll give it back later."

Debbie glanced from one male face to the other.

"And you need to tell me where all you've been since you bought this," Morgan added.

Behind them, the musicians began playing. Debbie pursed her lips and squinted, but released her hold on the bag. "I bought it over a week ago, in Yatesville. That afternoon, I went to the bookstore. Sunday was church, the Ranch, and church again. Monday was Prayer Shawl, then the church, and home. Tuesday I stayed home and did the family's laundry. Then Wednesday through Friday, I was in the clinic. Saturday, I went back to the bookstore. And Sunday again, church, Ranch, and church."

"You're sure you've been nowhere else?"

"I know, I live such an exciting life, it is difficult to keep it all straight."

"Sorry, Mom. It's important, though."

"You're a good man, Gabriel. You do what you need to do." Looking down into Hreno's face, Debbie whispered, "Let's go sit with those handsome horsemen."

The girls giggled and the three, accompanied by Bunny, walked away.

Tyler spoke quietly into his lapel pin, linked to Atticus' earpiece. Morgan notified his guards surrounding the compound. Gabriel headed back out of the sanctuary to the Sheriff's department after asking Morgan once again to play chauffer.

As Atticus concluded the service, he raised his hands, "I'm going to ask a favor of you. One for which I cannot give you an explanation until later. I'm going to ask you to go straight home. Over the next week, do not go out alone, and when you do, go out in groups, be vigilant, and cautious. And like your mother said, *don't talk to strangers*." He paused. "There will be a meeting of the elders immediately after the benediction."

After listening to Atticus's news, the elders began discussing the situation.

Doug took his arm from around Taralyn and stood. "How do we know it's not the work of some Earther killer? It's not like Dark soldiers have the monopoly on murder."

Tyler agreed, "We don't know. But Earther or alien, there is still a murderer in the vicinity, and we need to be concerned."

Ben stood, "What about the new Waystation?"

Matt replied, "It'll be a week before I can bulldoze the old barn, and another month to rebuild it, repair the house and build the clinic. And give me another two week's leighway."

Bea spoke up, "Plus, it's twenty miles between Black Creek and the Waystation. Ten miles in opposite directions from here."

Atticus paled. In his mind, he could still see the landing of Black Creek that afternoon all those years ago. By Bea's face, Atticus could tell she was seeing that area as it was thirty years earlier.

Morgan sighed, "We should have an identity of the victim tomorrow. That should help us determine a territory. The ME speculates this is a traveling serial killer. We should be able to trace his previous kills by Wednesday or Thursday. Right now, we should just be cautious."

Atticus stopped pacing. "The refugees will be confined to the compound. I think the horsemen and dog guards should stay confined to the Ranch as much as possible. Citizens of Morning Creek should continue normal activities, but just go in groups."

"So, we can hold the Prayer Shawl group tomorrow?" Ricean asked.

"I don't see why not. Morgan, you mind keeping an eye open for them?"

"It'd be my pleasure."

Taralyn giggled and Doug hid a grin. Tyler shook his head and smiled. "However, I think it might be best if you kept all the items you made to yourselves for a while. Just until we can determine how the victim got the cap."

"And, I know I don't need to say this, but I'm going to. This is not to be discussed with anyone or around anyone who is not an elder, until or unless I say otherwise."

After closing with a prayer, the elders went to retrieve their families who were waiting for them in the mess hall.

At the Ranch, Ben and Pierre waited while Wren-at-Dawn, Jeremy, Hreno and Venutha walked into the den.

Pierre sat on the armchair and Ben stood behind it.

Ben began, "There is to be no arguing on this matter."

Wren-at-Dawn and Jeremy exchanged worried glances. They hadn't broken any rules two weekends ago, but they hadn't discussed the events at the bar with Dad Ben or Pop Pierre either.

Pierre spoke softly, "We've moved the Waystation idea back to the middle of July."

"We were going to get the kittens," Hreno said.

"No discussion," Ben stated.

Hreno blinked.

Venutha sat up, "Daddy and Papa won't let them bulldoze until we've gotten the kittens, isn't that right, Daddy?" She smiled sweetly.

Ben scowled. She wasn't arguing; she was being compliant. He didn't know how to deal with Venutha being compliant.

"We promise," Pierre intervened. "Over the next week or two, no one is to go anywhere alone. We'll make sure the horsemen understand this, but it's up to you four to set the example. And Jeremy and Venutha, you'll need to make sure the horses and dogs know – no solitary rides or excursions anywhere for anyone."

Ben jumped in, "This is not open for debate."

"Alright, Daddy," Venutha said calmly.

Wren-at-Dawn and Jeremy exchanged glances again – suspicious ones this time.

"I have Prayer Shawl tomorrow morning, is that alright?" Hreno asked.

Venutha took her hand, "I'll go with you. And then you can go with me to the bookstore."

Wren-at-Dawn added, "We'll go with you to the bookstore, the four of us. Prayer Shawl will be held on sacred ground, the bookstore isn't. Safety in numbers, isn't that the idea?"

Venutha nodded agreeably, "I think that is a very wise idea, Wren-at-Dawn. Thank you."

Jeremy was not to be left out, "While we're there, we can get some books on how to live without electricity, just like the pioneers."

"The who?" Hreno asked.

"You can discuss that later," Ben held up a hand.

Venutha stated firmly, "Yes, Daddy."

Wren-at-Dawn repeated solemnly, "Yes, Daddy." Hreno and Jeremy nodded.

"Well, that's settled then." Ben patted Pierre on the shoulder.

"May the four of us go into the kennels and visit with Ohamaha a little bit? Then I promise we'll go straight to bed."

Pierre cocked his head at this sweet version of the queen.

"Why sure, Baby Girl," Ben melted.

They kissed and hugged the men goodnight and left.

"Did you see that? Not an ounce of defiance. I set the rules and she stuck by them. 'No argument' I said, and she was sweet as cream."

"Yep," Pierre rolled his eyes. "That was something."

"She's up to something, isn't she?"

"I'd stake my breakfast on it."

Ben sighed, "No argument there."

Gamga was in the kennel with his wife. He was playing with his latest litter when the four humans came in.

Venutha sat beside Ohamaha and kissed her head. The other three sat carefully, each taking a pup.

When everyone was settled, Venutha said, "Gamga was sitting with Joan during the elder's meeting. You're not going to believe what he heard! Tell us again, Gamga, and I'll translate."

The women of the Prayer Shawl group seemed nervous the next morning, but with the calming effect of the craft and Morgan refilling coffee mugs and playing with the children and the dogs and horses outside, the two hours flew and the women left feeling secure.

Gabriel had dropped Debbie off, not brooking any discussion of allowing her to ride her bike. He'd given her back the crochet bag and apologized for keeping the caps and yarn.

"Gabriel," Debbie patted his arm. "Everything is suspect in a murder investigation. I know, nothing is sacred. Don't worry about it. If it will help catch the killer, that's what's important."

So Gabriel dropped her off, surprised yet again by his mother-in-law. He didn't know she liked murder mystery books. She'd never mentioned it before. He waved at Morgan as he left.

Morgan took her and Bunny to the Mexican restaurant in town for lunch and then dropped them at her home. Bunny played with the boys and napped on the couch while Deborah finished an afghan.

The four Ranchers rode horses to the bookstore. At first, Venutha was very disappointed to hear that John Parker had called in sick. But Jeremy soon found books on living off the grid and the four spent the afternoon huddled together at a table, making plans.

20 ZARIS

Zaris stepped off the bus and looked around the town. He sniffed and his nose crinkled with the stench of Lambs of Light. He shouldered his pack, missing the feel of his crossbow and dagger at his side. Strategia Oscura Isabel Cortez had released him, but he still belonged to her. He was her assassin now, and he must obey her, no matter what: he'd prayed with her and they were now bound. Cortez took two weeks to train him in the ways of this world, and then sent him here, to track down the Redeemer. Zaris remembered Redeemer Stelt and his little girl Hreno. He was glad, if Cortez was right, and Stelt had found his girl again. It was only right to redeem weaves before they turned to despair. He'd seen a weave gone to darkness once. Terrible thing. Blighted the world and burnt everything in sight. His Strategia Oscuro had opened a door just in time, but Zaris would never forget the depth of the eternity he saw through the door which used to be a weave.

People nodded at Zaris in greeting as he walked through the streets. A few smiled at him, like they were clansmen or something closer. He nodded back, as Cortez had instructed him, but he couldn't bring himself to smile. These were Lambs of Light. Pitiless creatures who slaughtered their ways through his ranks; showing mercy to no one. They believed it was better to be dead than dark. Zaris took a deep breath and nodded at a beautiful young woman with white hair, blue eyes, and almond skin. Zaris took the chance at living every time he could. The tall bearded man next to the girl glared at Zaris and took her arm protectively.

Now, jealousy like that, Zaris understood. He looked back at the couple again and grinned.

"Atticus said not to be friendly with strangers, Lanza." The jealous man turned her away from Zaris's attention.

"Oh Wren-at-Dawn, I just smiled at him. Surely we can maintain our manners, even during this time?"

Zaris moved out of hearing and continued to reconnoiter the town. He'd need a place to stay; Cortez warned him that Earthers rarely slept outside. She gave him a wallet full of green paper and taught him how to use it to buy things like food and shelter. It didn't take him long to realize he could buy other things with it, too.

Zaris stopped, a scent of something familiar tweaked his nostrils. Darkness was near. It smelled good. He entered a building and stopped inside the door. Shelves of books filled the room. Zaris didn't read, none of his clansmen had ever even imagined the concept. But he remembered Stelt did. And there he was, the old redeemer himself, standing behind a counter smiling at a young girl. It was the girl from the picture Cortez had shown him, but she was not Stelt's weave.

Stelt frowned, sensing Zaris' darkness, and looked around to find the source.

Zaris nodded, a wry grin on his face, and stepped back outside into the street. The assassin turned into an alleyway and watched as Stelt came out into the street, still searching for the source of darkness he'd felt. The girl from the picture came out and took his elbow, speaking to him.

Zaris watched as the Redeemer shrugged and continued looking around. The couple he'd seen earlier walked up to Stelt and embraced the girl. The man nodded gruffly at Stelt, who bowed with a flourish. The beautiful girl beamed with goodness at the redeemer, and Zaris watched in disgust as the redeemer smiled in return.

21 EASTER BUNNY

"And you can cook squash with onions and a little bit of sugar so they scorch just right, or you can bake them with cream, or you can mix them with tomatoes and boil them, or you can dip them in batter and fry them until they are crispy yummy good! And," Bunny walked between Debbie and Morgan, holding their hands.

As Bunny took a breath, Morgan interrupted, "I only said they might have squash today, that's all I meant, Bunny."

"Yes, Uncle Owl. And it started me thinking about all the different kinds of squash and how they would taste. I never tasted squash before I came here. And I like it."

"On behalf of all the squash lovers of Earth," Debbie squeezed his hand, "I thank you!"

"What did you eat, before you came here?" Ever the soldier, Morgan wondered about the enemy's food supplies.

Bunny frowned and tensed his shoulders. "I had bread. Many types of bread, but not much at one time."

"Bunny," Debbie and her trio stopped at the doors of the Jamaican Me Hungry Mess Hall. "Remember the story about Pinocchio I told you last week?"

Bunny let go of her hand and rubbed his nose. "You should never never lie."

"So, all they fed you was bread," Morgan led.

Bunny nodded. Squaring his shoulders, he explained, "A warrior like my mother needs solid food – meat and vegetables and fruit. But me, one who she would need to redeem at any minute, why waste good food on me?"

Debbie trembled and Morgan squatted down to hold the boy's arms. Bunny smiled angelically at him, "Don't look so worried, Uncle Owl. I'm big and strong and if there's no squash today, then I'll eat grapes. I like grapes."

Morgan hugged him to his chest and Debbie rested her hand on the boy's head.

Bunny's lecture on the types of grapes and ways to prepare them only lasted to the buffet line. The heaping piles of vegetables gave him more than enough to talk about and he began describing each dish in great detail. Understandably, it slowed his progress through the line.

"You are taking too long!" a girl not much taller than Bunny pushed her way in front of him. "And you talk way too much."

"Easter!" her older sister Natalie yanked her backwards and into her proper place in line behind Debbie and Morgan. At Natalie's side (always at her side), Promise shook his finger at the girl and grinned.

Bunny stuck his tongue out and made a rude noise.

Easter responded in kind.

Promise flashed his hands signals at Natalie, who roared with laughter. "Easter Bunny, behave!" she translated out loud.

The people who heard it, laughed.

Bunny stopped and looked around. He whispered, "Why do they laugh?"

Easter crossed her arms, "Because they're stupid."

"Don't be rude," Debbie said firmly to Easter.

"Yeah," Bunny pointed at the people, "Don't be rude. It's not nice to laugh at me that way. Or at that Easter girl."

Morgan pushed ahead and plopped two round disks on Bunny's plate. "Here, take some pancakes and go find us a table."

Bunny looked at the disks and tears filled his eyes. "It's bread. You gave me bread, Uncle Owl."

"No. No, Bunny, it's not bread. It's pancakes." Morgan and Debbie assured him together.

"I don't like pancakes. They're for babies." Easter sashayed around them and headed for an empty table.

"Hey, Bunny. You want to make Easter mad? Go sit with her." Natalie grinned.

"But I don't want to make her mad."

The older girl touched his shoulder, "You haven't been around many children, have you."

Debbie's nostrils flared. Morgan took Bunny's plate, "Come on, son. Let's go sit down and start eating."

They sat next to Easter who looked surprised at first, and then pleased.

Bunny whispered, "I have been around children. Many children. But not free ones. Only ones about to be turned to despair."

Debbie kissed his forehead, "Eat your breakfast, Bunny."

Easter looked terrified, then as she watched Bunny, her expression changed to one of pity.

Bunny turned and spoke softly to Morgan, "Why does she stare at me?"

Easter squeaked and blushed.

"Eat your breakfast," Morgan said softly.

"Here," Easter plopped a round orange ball onto Bunny's plate. "These are cantaloupe. It sounds like what a horse would do, but it isn't. It's good. The whole thing is big, but they cut them into these tiny little balls. I like them."

Bunny picked up the juicy fruit and sniffed it.

"You can lick it if you want to, just to see what it tastes like before you put the whole thing in your mouth. In case you don't like it and have to spit it out. I had to do that with brussel sprouts once."

Bunny licked it and grinned. The whole globe squished inside his mouth and he laughed.

"I like these!" Bunny picked up a wad of hash browns and placed it on Easter's plate. "But I don't like to put that red stuff on it like Uncle Owl does."

Easter grinned and picked it up with her fingers. It disappeared into her mouth with a satisfied smacking sound.

The two children shared their plates equally, until there was just the pancakes left.

Easter looked at them and up at Bunny. He was glaring at them in dismay. "Pancakes aren't for babies. Honest. I lied. They're good."

"You lied?" Bunny whispered.

"Yeah. I'm sorry. "

"Is your nose going to grow?"

"I'm not Pinocchio!"

They giggled.

Easter reached over and poured some blue syrup onto his plate. "They're OK. Sort of like sweet bread, but they're really good with blueberry syrup."

Bunny looked at his plate again. Easter reached over and broke a triangle off of the circle. She put it in her mouth and smacked. Then she reached across and broke off a triangle and put it toward Bunny's face. He tentatively leaned forward and took a bite. Squealing with glee, he broke off a triangle and fed it to Easter. The pancakes were gone, leaving behind two very happy children smeared with blueberry syrup.

22 BLACK CREEK

Lanza looked over at the man standing by the door of the church. She'd seen him several times around town, but today, as he leaned against the visitors' pedestal just inside the door, he seemed to be in pain. He was sweating and his shoulders were hunched protectively over his abdomen. She watched as he took a deep shaky breath and glanced up at her again. Hoping to heal him, she began to sing.

Tears streamed down the man's face as she sang another line of an ancient hymn. He shuddered and his flesh beneath his eyes and the hallows of his cheeks darkened. She sang louder, imbuing the words with power and light.

He held up a hand in supplication and mouthed silently, "Please!" Then he turned and exited the tiny chapel next to the old cemetery.

Lanza had come to practice at the old chapel with her friend Dryesillia, who often accompanied her on a silver bowl. Dryesillia had gone to the restroom a while ago. She should be back any moment. The Elders had impressed on them the need to stay in groups.

She heard the man sob and cry out again, "Please."

Thinking only of providing help, Lanza followed. She had no way of knowing that Dryesillia lay in a stupor on the marble floor, knocked unconscious by the same man who was laying a trap for her.

The pain lessened the farther Zaris moved away from the sanctuary, although his feet were still burned by the holy ground on which they trod. The girl with the white hair and beautiful blue eyes was following him. If he could get her to the car – the car he'd stolen from Stelt – the first part of his plan would be complete and the agony he'd suffered by being inside such a place of light would be worth it.

He slumped over the hood and waited for her to approach. He mustn't let her sing. He'd never experienced this particular weaponry until his last Strategia Oscuro – his late Strategia Oscuro - had brought him to this world. He was amazed by it; sung with purity and conviction, one note could splinter a dark soldier's mind. From the back of a forbidden portion in his thoughts, he remembered that his mother used to sing to him as he went to sleep. She was a good person, a sweet loving person. He wondered if she still thought of him. She would have liked the song this young woman was singing. Lanza was almost beside him now. He felt her hand touch his elbow. He struck the flat heel of his hand against her larynx and threw her into the convertible as she collapsed.

Zaris drove the car directly to the creek. It took a while to travel the ten miles, so he talked to the girl as her breaths gurgled around the crushed larynx. She was unconscious, but he always felt the need to explain to his victims the reason he had to assassinate them. It was only fair that they should know, in their last minutes, why those were their last minutes.

"My name is Assassin, but my mother called me Zaris. You would have liked my mother. I want you to know, you have done nothing to warrant assassination. You are a means to an end, that's all. I've been watching Redeemer Stelt since I got here. He fits right in. He fits in too well. My Strategia Oscura Cortez said that I needed to stir things up enough so Stelt feels scared; feels like he needs to escape these Lambs of Light. If he escapes, he'll take his little girl with him. And then, once he's away from such powerfully holy ground, my Strategia Oscura can come and take them both.

"Understand, this isn't a usual job for an Assassin of my caliber. But I belong to Strategia Oscura Cortez, and I do what she commands. So I've been watching him, and I have been watching you. You are very popular. People love you. So I worked out a plan where I can use my skills and follow my Strategia Oscura's command at the same time.

"And if this isn't enough to scare him into running, it'll be enough evidence to get him back in Strategia Oscura Cortez's hands. See, this is his car, and you'll leave enough of your blood and vomit in it, and I took these scissors directly from his apron at the store he works in. These are what I'm going to kill you with."

The girl whimpered and tried to wake up.

"I promise, it'll only hurt just a little, and death will come quickly. And I'll not desecrate your body living or dead." He pulled into the dirt road leading down to the picnic area beside Black Creek.

He kept his promise.

"Careful!" Wren-at-Dawn put out an arm, blocking the path ahead of his housemates. White splatter and dark brown scat spotted the peach orchard as a flying mass of scales, claws and wings cast a dark shadow along the tree line.

Hreno put her hand over her nose and mouth. "Who would have thought that dragons smelled so bad!"

"He's old, and sick. His kidneys aren't working properly," Jeremy supplied.

"From what Flowers-on-a-Vine-at-Midnight says," Venutha grinned wickedly, "that's not the only thing about Scarlet-Sun-Rising-Across-the-Desert that is old and isn't working properly."

Wren-at-Dawn took a calming breath, trying not to succumb to giggles like Hreno and Jeremy.

The object of their discussion landed with a grunt and flapped his large tattered wings. The sound of boulders tumbling down a mountain came out of his open mouth. Venutha roared something in return and pointed at the rows of watermelons across the field. Scarlet-Sun-Rising-Across-the-Desert nodded and ambled toward them. The dragoneers held their noses as the old sire passed gas with every other step.

"Well, does Flowers-on-a-Vine-at-Midnight at least like Scarlet-Sun-Rising-Across-the-Desert?" Hreno asked.

"Oh yeah, she likes him real well." Jeremy led them to the peach trees. "He's the only male she's ever seen. She has a great sense of humor. She keeps saying he's hot and then laughs and laughs."

"Dragon humor," Wren-at-Dawn smiled.

"So, if she likes him, once he gets better…" Hreno left her question open.

"They're," Jeremy reached up and plucked a peach. "They're not quite sure how it's done."

Wren-at-Dawn began picking peaches, too. "Some of the mares are going into heat. If we could bring them here, with the stallions of their choices, the dragons could – you know – watch."

"Do dragons and horses do things the same way?" Hreno dropped peaches into her sack.

"Yes," Venutha stated firmly. "Otka told me."

"Otka – watched?" Wren-at-dawn paled.

"Well, it takes dragons longer than horses. Three or four days sometimes." Venutha tilted her head back and bellowed a sound like a waterfall. Flowers-on-a-Vine-at-Midnight rushed over their heads and swooped down. The female dragon landed gracefully beside her yet-to-be mate. He looked up at her and placed a large watermelon gently into her open mouth. She purred and watermelon juice sprayed them both. Scarlet began purring, too.

"Sounds like it's starting," Hreno smiled and took Jeremy's hand.

"We'd probably better head back to the farmhouse. Otka says dragons lose all sense of where they are once they start rolling around." Venutha shouldered one of the bags of peaches and the four headed home.

Jeremy and Hreno leaped up the steps and onto the porch. Venutha waited on Wren-at-Dawn, who had turned to watch the sun set over their fields. She brushed a mosquito off his arm and smiled up at him. He looked dreamy, "I love it here."

She nodded in total agreement.

Wren-at-Dawn grunted and clutched at his old scar. His hand came away crimson with blood as he sank to his knees. He heard Venutha screaming for help, but was too lost in the weaving to understand. He was bleeding, but it wasn't his blood. He knew without a doubt that the blood flowing from his scar belonged to Lanza. Wren-at-Dawn grabbed Venutha, yanking her to the ground beside him. "Lanza," he gasped. "Lanza is dying."

Venutha nodded repeatedly and then cradled Wren-at-Dawn's head in her arms. The bleeding had stopped before Jeremy could explain the situation to Doug by cell phone.

"Hreno, help me get him into the house." Venutha staggered under Wren-at-Dawn's weight. The three of them wrestled him up the stairs and onto the porch. Hreno returned with a bowl of water and towels.

Jeremy gently removed his shirt and examined the wound. Blotting away the blood, he spoke softly, as if to one of his horses. "They've called for a lock down at the refuge. All children will be accounted for in their dorms. The gates will be closed. The sheriff's deputies will be searching the town. They'll find Lanza. Doug promised."

"In darkness. She died in a place of darkness. Lanza died. She's dead."

Venutha rocked him as he sobbed, kissing his forehead.

"You're not bleeding anymore." Jeremy took out his stethoscope and listened to Wren-at-Dawn's chest.

"Not my blood. Not mine."

Hreno placed her hand on his knee. "How did she die?"

Wren-at-Dawn shook his head. "I don't know."

Jeremy looped his arm around his friend's waist. "Let's get him inside. He'll need a clean shirt. There's enough hot water for a bath. We should hear something soon."

"I'll fix a pot of tea. Grandmother Debbie says a pot of tea can cure most ills." Hreno headed for the kitchen.

"Venutha, go get him some clean clothes, and another towel."

"I'm not leaving him."

"I'm going to put him into the bath tub."

"I'll bathe him. You know where his clothes are better than me."

"He's a guy!"

"He's Wren-at-Dawn. He needs me."

"Well," Jeremy let go of Wren-at-Dawn once they helped him into the tub. He stood at the door and watched Venutha turn on the spigot and gently wash the blood from the young man's chest and abdomen.

"Bring me a gown, too." She stepped into the tub and blood ran down her shirt as well.

Stelt watched his daughter while the poppies blew among the gravestones. He was safe in the crowd, one of the hundreds of mourners who had come to pay their respects for the fallen singer. Hreno was crying, but had not given in to despair. He was afraid she might; he was afraid he'd have to redeem her, after all this time, when she was now so happy and beautiful. Jeremy stood at her right side, his arm around her waist. Stelt would normally have raged against such familiarity, but he had also grown to admire the young man who spoke to animals and healed them. Beside Jeremy stood Wren-at-Dawn. His grief was like a mask over the Horseman's face, darkening it, aging it with indelible lines of sorrow. Stelt had once felt the same, when Hreno's mother was killed. Stelt watched the Horseman battle against despair and worried for him, too. Beside the Horseman stood his little friend Venutha. She looked precious, like a bud about to blossom. Her eyes never left Wren-at-Dawn's face; her hand never left his arm.

Atticus spoke, "Revelation is a collection of letters from one of the Bringers of Light of Jesus, the Son of God to the early churches. Revelation 2:10 begins, *Do not fear what you are about to suffer.* It ends with, *Be faithful unto death, and I will give you the crown of life.*"

A baby squalled and was quickly hushed by her mother's embrace.

"The scriptures do not say, Don't fear what you might or might not suffer. The Apostle John stated it correctly; you are going to suffer. This field is full of people who have known suffering. It's not a possibility; it's a reality. There is suffering in this world, and on all other worlds where Soldiers of the Light battle to hold back the dark.

"To each of us, God has given gifts – strengths and skills. I look across this field and see staffs and swords and archers and dog guards and horsemen." Here he nodded at Wren-at-Dawn. "I see musicians and prayer warriors and dreamwalkers. And I see singers. Like Lanza."

Atticus paced as was his habit to do when he got to the heart of his sermons. "Lanza of the Itarri, daughter of Jagty and Markir, was fifteen when the Darkness discovered her world. Like Earth, Itarra had had rumors of Dark soldiers for centuries, but suddenly, one winter day, the Darkness opened doors of despair all over her world and consumed it. Portals of light also began opening, and Lanza found herself stepping through to another world. For three years, Lanza and her people traveled from world to world seeking sanctuary. She found it here, at the Refuge.

"And here, under Patsy's tutorage, she discovered her love for singing could be developed into an incredible force for good. She. Was. Remarkable. And more than that, she was kind. And more than that, she was loved. And more than that, she served the light, the bringers of the light, and the light eternal."

The people gathered there murmured *Selah* or *Amen*.

"Lanza was faithful. She was faithful unto death. She suffered. And she died. But she was faithful unto death. And today, she is wearing the Crown of Life in heaven."

"Selah!" Hreno's voice was strong as tears streamed down her face.

"Amen," Atticus nodded at the dragoneers.

The choir began to sing, "When peace like a river attends my path, and sorrows like sea billows roll." The congregants joined in to complete the song. Stelt had never heard such a sorrowful song filled with light in every word. He had never understood how someone could live through despair and not become engulfed by it. But these people had. He found himself humming along with the second verse.

The body of Lanza was lowered into the grave among the poppies in the hot August heat.

Stelt felt eyes on him. There, at the back of the crowd, the Assassin watched him, grinning. Stelt remembered the man from his last battalion – the one he belonged to when he first came to Earth. Zaris the Assassin killed like a Lamb of Light – quickly and without a chance of survival. Zaris taught Redeemers how to kill swiftly. He took no pleasure in killing; he was just really good at it.

Stelt felt his skin go cold with the realization – Zaris had killed Lanza, because of him. Cortez must have found him and used Zaris to draw him out. It was his fault that the Horseman's woman was dead.

Zaris nodded at Stelt. Stelt glared in return and backed his way out of the crowd. He'd have to run now; he'd have to leave his little girl and run. He'd not go back to Strategia Oscura Cortez and to her darkness. He wanted – Stelt gasped – he wanted to return to the Light. But first, Stelt needed to avenge the death of Lanza at Zaris' hands. In killing Zaris, Stelt was sure that he could keep Hreno hidden, safe from Cortez's reach. If Zaris had told her their location, she would have been here. There would have been no need to kill the Singer. No need to break the heart of the Horseman. Yes, one more *eye for an eye* as the Light of this world spoke of in the Bible. And then Stelt could be done with the Darkness.

23 THE DRAGONEERS

Morgan pulled his Forrester up behind the massive truck and shut off the engine. Bunny counted to five and then unbuckled his seat belt. Debbie looked for something in Morgan's eyes and then sighed. She got out of the car and the three of them walked up to the four dragoneers climbing out of the truck. Hreno was pale, Jeremy smiled, Venutha nodded and followed Wren-at-Dawn up onto the porch.

"The livingroom is pretty, but the kitchen is more comfortable. Let's go in there and we can all have iced tea," Venutha suggested. She took Wren-at-Dawn's hand. The rest of them followed silently.

Wren-at-Dawn sat at his normal place at the head of the table, Morgan sat opposite him. The others sat around the table and Venutha began filling glasses from the massive crock on the counter. She handed them around and Jeremy got up and placed a box of cookies on the table. Bunny was the only one who took a cookie, but they all sipped the cool tea.

Morgan took a deep breath and sighed. "We need to talk."

The dragoneers waited. In the distance they could hear the sounds of boulders crashing into the sea – or dragons having an evening chat.

"Debbie and Bunny are going to move in with you," Morgan began.

"We're fine by ourselves," Wren-at-dawn stated.

"You may be," Morgan nodded, "but Debbie isn't. And since Bunny won't go anywhere without Debbie, you get him, too."

"What do you mean, I'm not fine?" Debbie frowned. "I thought I was coming here to help them. They don't need any reverse psychology crap at a time like this."

Morgan's eyebrows raised. Debbie squared her shoulders and glared.

"We're just fine by ourselves, honest." Venutha got up to refill her glass.

"But Debbie's not," Morgan's voice was calm.

Wren-at-Dawn pierced Debbie with a look. "Because she's linked to the killer."

"I'm what?"

"Linked. You know him. Or he knows you. That's what Atticus said."

"Atticus talked to you about this?" Morgan frowned.

Wren-at-dawn opened his mouth, then glanced at Venutha. She reddened.

"The dogs told you," Debbie said.

The dragoneers nodded.

"Well, they didn't tell me, so please fill me in. How exactly am I linked to a deranged serial killer?"

"The crocheted cap on the first victim," Morgan said.

"The *girly girl* pink one," Hreno's voice was soft.

"The one someone stole out of my bag."

"Yes. And the scissors that were used on the second victim."

"On Lanza," Wren-at-Dawn whispered.

"The murder weapon," Jeremy had to clear his voice. He put his hand over Hreno's elbow and she gripped his fingers.

"Yes. They belonged to Debbie."

"Also stolen from my bag."

"Debbie had nothing to do with the murders. She was affected by both of them – with witnesses during those times," Morgan assured them. "However, the cap and the scissors came out of her bag – stolen – within a day or two of the first murder. So she knows or is known by the killer."

"Monster," Bunny grabbed another cookie and crawled into Debbie's lap. "I will never leave you, Grandmother Debbie. I can feel when monsters and assassins are near. I'll keep you safe."

"Assassins?" Hreno paled further. "There was an assassin in my father's battalion. I don't remember his name, but if he escaped, he might have found the Refuge."

"An assassin wouldn't kill a stranger. The first woman wasn't a refugee. She had nothing to do with the Refuge. And as I recall, assassins don't take hours torturing someone. They kill outright." Wren-at-Dawn shook his head. "As for Lanza, what Strategia Oscuro would want her dead over any of the rest of us?"

"Assassin?" Morgan asked.

"They are rare. Like a weave, only a few Strategia Oscuro have them. They train Redeemers how to quickly kill their weaves, should the need arise. They are usually sent to kill the weaves of other Strategia Oscuro, so those can't gather children from other worlds." Hreno explained.

"And Lanza wasn't a weave. It would have served no purpose for a Strategia Oscuro to order her death." Wren-at-Dawn forced himself to remain calm. "Except, if it were an assassin, he might have mistaken Lanza for me."

The table was teeming with unspoken reassurances that would have meant nothing to the man.

Jeremy cleared his throat again. "I don't understand why you can't find him. Owahah said you knew what kind of car he drove."

"A car? What car?" Debbie shifted Bunny back onto his chair.

"Owahah didn't know; dogs don't describe colors or makes of cars very well."

"But, if you know the car, you could track the owner. Even I know that," Venutha insisted.

"The car belonged to a woman in Tennessee. The woman was murdered and the car stolen over eight months ago."

Jeremy reached for a cookie. "If you recognized the car enough to trace it, someone around here knows who drives it. I mean, there's just not that many cars in the area. What did it look like?"

"Red Chrysler LaBaron convertible."

The people at the table gasped collectively.

"What?" Morgan didn't sound surprised. "You know this car?"

"You stupid clandestine need-to-know-only cloak-and-dagger top-secret home-guard conspiracy-theory machinating ASS!"

"Debbie!" Morgan's mouth gaped in shock.

"Why didn't you tell me about this car?"

"You recognize it?"

"We all do," Jeremy stated.

"I don't! Whose car is it?" Hreno asked.

"It can't be. John wouldn't murder anyone," Venutha shouted.

Wren-at-Dawn stood.

"John, John who?" Morgan had his iPhone out.

"John Parker, the book store guy," Debbie's mouth felt dry. "The man who looked like a coyote."

"But no! I saw him at the funeral. He was crying, too!" Venutha gasped.

"In the movies, they always look through the crowd at the funeral because the murderer shows up – to gloat."

"Jeremy," Debbie spoke softly. "That's not helping."

Morgan turned his phone to Debbie. "Is this him?"

She tilted her head, focusing. "It's hard to tell. But I think so."

"Venutha knows him well. Let her see." Jeremy grabbed the phone.

"He's not like that." She stood and looked at Wren-at-Dawn, refusing the phone. "He's not like that. He wouldn't torture or kill anyone."

"He didn't torture Lanza." Morgan assured the boy.

"He didn't kill her, either! Listen to me! He goes to church with us. He knows us – he knows all about us!"

"You told him about us," Wren-at-dawn's voice was ice.

"No, no – he told me! He told me all about Hreno and what a good girl she was. He told me about her first; he knew that we are best-friends."

"Morgan, serial killers don't change their methods except to accelerate the torture." Debbie was ignored. "Sit down! Everyone – sit down and hush. This is a very emotional time, but you are all going to have to calm down and think logically. Center yourselves. Pray if that's what it takes, but shut up and think!"

They blinked, and then they sat back down and listened. Hreno picked up Morgan's phone, staring into the screen.

"This is what we know. There have been two women murdered. One was tortured and slowly killed. Various weapons of torture were used. The killer left a trophy – my pink cap – on her head. The second woman was not tortured. She was quickly killed and then the murder weapon – the only weapon – was left at the scene. The cap and the scissors were stolen out of my bag at the same time. They disappeared on the same day – I assume taken by the same person. The car was well-known to us – belonging to a friend of Venutha's. It was well-known because it was so recognizable."

"It was a great-looking car," Jeremy agreed.

"The first killer knew me – or at least stole the cap and the scissors from me. And since I knew John and often sat at the bookstore where he worked, chances are he took the cap and the scissors."

"He didn't kill!"

Morgan held up a silencing hand. "Go on, Debbie."

"Serial killers escalate. The first murder was viciously horrible. Each wound was made to prolong the woman's suffering. The second was clean, swift, and merciful. He clipped the artery in her groin and she bled out in minutes. Totally different. And connected, not to me, but to John."

"But two different killers."

"Two different killers," Debbie agreed with Morgan.

"Connected to me." Hreno's face was wet with tears. "To me. They killed Lanza because of me."

Morgan came up onto the porch with a bottle he'd taken out of his car. He held it up to Debbie and smiled sadly, "I thought we might could use something stronger than iced tea."

She hesitated, put down the shawl she was crocheting, and held out her glass.

He poured the golden liquid into both glasses, sat beside her and put the bottle on the wicker table between them. They watched a huge dark form rise from the horizon and soar across the starlit sky.

"I do believe that was a dragon."

Debbie sighed, the huffed a soft laugh.

"Beats the hell out of lions and tigers and bears."

"I'm still mad at you."

"You have a right to be." He clinked his glass against hers on the table. "Maybe more than you know."

"I think praying with Atticus makes ya'll stupid."

"Now you're just being rude."

"You knew who owned that car."

"Yes. Le'Vander recognized it."

"And you put that poor child through it anyway."

"Stelt was supposed to have been in a high security prison run by one of my own people. The fact that he had tracked us down and has been living among us for months meant that my people were no longer trustworthy. And if my IIA staff has been compromised by the Dark, everything we've worked for could be destroyed. We had to be sure."

"And now you are."

"The prison is empty. They've been moved somewhere; I don't know where."

They watched as another dragon, smaller with tattered wings, eclipsed the moon.

"So how long will we be imprisoned here?"

"We're keeping you safe here."

"Really? Safe from whom?"

"From Bunny's mother, from Hreno's father Stelt, and the commander who was supposed to have them both in custody."

"Stelt lived in Morning Creek since before I moved here. If he betrayed our where-abouts to your commander, he never acted on it."

"She," Morgan growled. "Isabel Cortez is a woman."

Something about the way Morgan said her name made Debbie pause. She shrugged, "Stelt never hurt us. And he had plenty of opportunity to."

"He's a redeemer. You of all people know what that means."

"Me?"

He looked away from her.

"What the hell do you know about me?"

He faced her. "Everything. It took a lot of work, but I found out about your childhood."

"That's none of your business. And you've changed the subject."

He refreshed their glasses from the bottle. "What was the subject?"

"Why we're here."

"I told you – to keep you safe."

She glared at him in silence.

"OK, Debbie. You tell me why you're here."

"The children are being held hostage so their parents will stay in line."

"What?" he exploded. "Have you lost your mind?"

"Who rebelled against Atticus five years ago?"

"What?"

"Five years ago – The Battle of Crystal Lake. Bea told me it nearly split the church. And it nearly killed Atticus – the betrayal of his right hand man Rutger Perkins."

"That's not exactly," Morgan hesitated.

"Dr. Ben, Joan, Pierre, you, my son-in-law."

"And Rutger, Patsy, Le'Vander and Taralyn. I was there. These children and Mitchell were there, too."

"Mitchell, the crazy priest who turns into a white buffalo."

"He does what?"

"It doesn't matter. What matters is that almost all of the people who rebelled against Atticus have someone they love living here."

"We weren't rebels. Joan and I weren't even part of it. We were there and they joined us there."

"Doesn't change the facts that Atticus has now placed these children – and now me! – here under guard to keep our loved ones in line."

Morgan stood. "That's ludicrous!"

Fire streaked across the sky. A dragon roared and belched fire again.

"And putting four teenagers on a farm ten miles from anywhere without adult supervision isn't ludicrous?"

"They're not normal teens. They're trustworthy."

"Trustworthy rebels, that's interesting."

"They can talk to dragons. They're needed here. And Wren-at-Dawn is an adult. And now you're here."

"Yeah, me and Bunny. Way out in the wilderness with a crazy serial killer chasing Hreno and Bunny's mom is still out there, sharpening her knife. You love Bunny, and I know you care about me. You care about us enough to keep you in line, too."

"You're not looking at this the right way."

"The right way? Or Atticus' way?"

Morgan stopped. His shoulders tensed and his face clouded. Then he looked at her. "That's really pretty yarn. What are you making?" as if they hadn't been talking about rebellions and serial killers and dragons.

"You're brain-washed, Morgan. Why can't you – you of all people – understand this?"

He sat beside her. "It's not like that. It's not brain-washing. It's a choice. I choose to belong to Atticus. My choice. If you'd just pray with him."

"And become pregnant and fight the Darkness on alien worlds. Gosh, do you think I could meet Luke Skywalker?"

"I told him you'd never trust anyone."

"I trust people."

"Bullshit."

"I trust you."

"To a point. A very small point."

"Well what choice do I have? When I ask you a question that makes you think outside of the church, you get all glassy-eyed and start quoting country music."

Morgan snorted and then bellowed with laughter. "I trained the elders to do that. To side-step awkward questions, we just change subjects totally. Most people don't notice it. They just get distracted to the new subject."

"So, in your opinion, I don't trust anyone AND I'm stupid."

"I don't think you're stupid. But you are blind. Blind to what's really going on here. Blind because of what your father did."

"Leave my father out of this!" Her hand slipped unconsciously to her left shoulder.

"Your father was a redeemer. You're a weave, Debbie. A weave! Like Bunny and Hreno and Wren-at-Dawn. And like Wren-at-Dawn, your father tried to kill you. To redeem you."

"That's a lie!" She jumped up, her crochet falling from her lap. "My father loved me!"

"Of course he loved you. But when he heard voices telling him to sacrifice you, he thought it was God. And he loved God more than he loved you."

"No! No, no, no!" She wrapped her arms around her head and sobbed. Morgan embraced her within seconds. She fought him, shoved him away and ran off the porch only to stand in the driveway with her arms outstretched. Her head lolled back and she howled. Overhead, the dragon's song overwhelmed the sound of her sobs.

Morgan stepped behind her, not touching, speaking softly. "Your mother walked into a portal of light when you were young. For five years, everyone thought your father had killed your mother and hidden the body. It broke him; he lost himself to despair. And somehow, the darkness told him to kill you. But he had lost his mind. He thought the voices came from God. So one Sunday morning, he called you up in front of his congregation and plunged a knife into your chest. He left you for dead and ran into the woods. You were taken in by one of the women who had come to spend the summer as a missionary but your father refused to allow you to be adopted. He died in prison when you were sixteen, and then you changed your name to Smith.

"You're a weave, Debbie. You opened a portal and your mother walked through it to another world. Your father was your redeemer. You're one of us. God sent you to us – arranged

Gabriel's being on duty at Crystal Lake five years ago. It all led to you being here."

"Why?" her voice was raspy soft. "Why would God want me?"

Morgan turned her to face him. "The same reason God wants any of us – to hold back the dark."

Wren-at-Dawn heard Jeremy's footsteps leading onto the sleeping porch. He turned slightly and smiled, "Dragons are really loud tonight."

"They're singing. I think it's a mating song." Jeremy stood next to his hero and looked out over the balcony to the stars above.

"Singing. Maybe dragons are the ones who taught Venutha to sing."

The boys smiled at each other.

"There! Do you see him? He's flying in from the west, under her. He's saying that he's the night wind, come to bring her gentle relief from the dry and weary day."

"Dragons are rather poetic, aren't they," Wren-at-Dawn sighed.

"I guess, lonely as they've been, it just comes out as poetry."

"Here they come!" The dragons flew wing-tip to wing-tip and barely cleared the farmhouse roof. They pivoted and soared back over. The sound of rocks bouncing into a crevasse filled the air.

"What did they say now, Venutha?" The two girls stepped onto the sleeping porch, arm in arm.

"You are my shadow, you are my sunshine. You are the water that sprays from the wildest waterfall."

Jeremy grinned, "Now he's singing. You are life and lovely and gentleness and kindness, but you will guard our children like the night sky guards the stars."

"The night sky guards the stars?" Hreno pulled Venutha into the space between the two boys.

"I think that's what he said."

"Yeah. But maybe it meant something different," Venutha brushed her elbow against Wren-at-Dawn.

"What else are they saying?" he asked.

"She's saying, our nest will be filled with eggs, and each will hatch into the light and remain in the light as long as the light reigns."

Jeremy continued, "Now he's saying, we have found paradise, a land promised to us by God. Filled with fruit and wonders and safety."

"They're singing about us, about this place," Hreno whispered. "Do you think? Do you think God gave this place to them?"

"I think," Wren-at-Dawn slipped his arm around Venutha's shoulders and cupped Hreno's cheek in his palm. "I think that one day soon, the skies will be filled with dragons, because of us. Because God chose us to give them a place of sanctuary."

A glob of bright white spun down towards them from the pair of dragons. It splatted on the eaves just above them, dousing them all with white matter that reeked of sulphur.

"Quick! In here!" Jeremy pushed them into the small bathroom and turned on the shower. They began laughing and then couldn't stop laughing as they bathed each other. Soap, shampoo, and warm water washed away the guano. Laughter and hugs washed away the grief.

They toweled off and returned to watch the mating pair of dragons in flight, well back behind the roof line. Then they all piled onto the double beds in the boys' room – which they quietly pushed together - and talked for hours. They awoke feeling safe and warm, in each other's arms.

24 A PROPITIATION FOR SIN

Gwen had had a restless night. No one she knew could have slept well after the murders of this summer and Lanza's funeral two days ago. She kissed her husband as he read his email and got their children ready for Morning Meadow. She supervised all the warriors now, but felt she wasn't needed this morning. Not like at the beginning. The children under their care had already successfully waged battles against the Dark on various worlds. She was tired of waging war. She was tired of death and savagery and preparing children to kill and die.

And she was pregnant again.

She moved through the ranks of children learning and mastering Morning Meadow, Mountain Wall and the Lightening Bolts. The Voices were silent this morning, and would be all week, in observance of mourning for Lanza. Gwen bowed her head as Mitchell closed the exercises with prayer.

Visolela touched her arm. Visolela, so kind and gentle and Gwen's spiritual sister. She didn't ask – she didn't have to – she just pulled Gwen into an embrace and they clung to each other.

"I want to go pray."

Visolela nodded.

"Not here. I can't think here. There are too many-"

"Demands?"

Gwen nodded.

"Go. I'll take our children to breakfast and then they can play in the nursery."

"Atticus said not to go alone."

"Now you start listening to your husband?" Visolela laughed. "If the Warrior of Atticus is not safe alone, then no one is safe here among the Refuge. Where will you go?"

"The old sanctuary."

Again Visolela nodded.

The guard at the gates saluted and let her out. She walked the two miles to her old house through the pastureland and pecan groves. She felt like she was walking through jello but didn't recognize the sensation until just beside the cement angel. The key was missing. The doors were wide open. Her cell phone vibrated against her thigh, but she ignored it. She could feel the desecration to the church – to her beautiful little church with Matthew, Mark, Luke and John in stained glass on one side, Grace, Joy, Hope and Charity on the other, and Jesus-on-the-cross behind the altar.

There wasn't much blood. Gwen thought fleetingly that perhaps the blood had seeped into the wooden boards and been swallowed by the earth below as a sacrifice.

A propitiation for sin, the thought came unbidden and hauntingly familiar to her mind. A wave of nausea swept up and over Gwen and she vomited beside the first pew.

She forced her way forward and examined the body. One large wound beside the sternum and below the collar bone testified as cause of death. It was a clean wound, deep and sure to have punctured the heart. *Swift. A swift and merciful death.* The victim's eyes were open and there was blood on his chin. His lips were parted. His mouth was filled with blood.

Without thinking. Gwen grasped his jaw in her right hand. His tongue had been removed. In its place was a wadded up piece of paper. She pulled it out and opened it. It was page 2180 from the altar Bible and Romans 13:11, 12 and the first part of 13 had been circled: *Besides this you know the time, that the hour has come for you to wake from sleep. For salvation is nearer to us now than when we first believed. The night is far gone, the day is at hand. So then let us cast off the works of darkness and put on the armor of light. Let us walk properly as in the daytime.*

25 THE WEAVES

"I don't think I will ever get the smell of dragon out of my nostrils," Jeremy rubbed his nose vigorously against his sleeve.

Hreno laughed and stopped. "Here," she pulled a twist of jasmine from the vine along the fence. Crushing the blossoms, she dabbed them against his upper lip. He gently cupped her elbows; she moved even closer. His eyes twinkled as he bent his head towards hers. The kiss that almost was turned into a sneeze. Hreno jumped backwards with a squawk and Jeremy felt mortified.

Across the fields, Grandma Debbie rang the dinner triangle hanging from the front porch.

Hreno reddened and stammered, "Bunny is fixing mushroom soup."

"Yeah, he wouldn't shut up about it."

Hreno bobbed her head. "I wish you weren't going tomorrow," her words rushed out. "I know you have to go, and this is your last year, and I'm sure you have lots of friends there and they missed you this summer but I still – I don't – I like the way you – well, I just –"

Jeremy grinned. He placed his palms on her shoulders and brought her closer again. This time, nothing in the world would have stopped them. Their lips met and their breath mingled. The friendship and camaraderie that bound them gave them courage to hold each other close and linger over their first kiss. A mosquito feasted unnoticed on Hreno's ankle. The triangle jangled again, and the dragoneers continued their embrace.

Behind them, Wren-at-Dawn cleared his throat with no response. Finally, Venutha flung her arms around them, "Stop already!! You're going to have to breathe sometime!!"

Wren-at-Dawn tried to look solemn, but then burst into laughter and joined in the hugs. The foursome wrestled playfully with each other up the path to the house.

"Oh!" Venutha stopped, "I forgot to check on the kittens. Momma Cat moved them into the barn last night; I wanted to make sure they were safe."

"I'll go! I'd love to see the little calico one again," Hreno offered.

"I'll go with you," Jeremy smiled.

"No." Wren-at-Dawn stated firmly. "If you two got into that barn, I'd have to answer to Papa Pierre."

"Wren-at-Dawn!" Hreno blushed.

"That's not what we were going to do!" Jeremy assurance lacked conviction.

"I wouldn't want to do it in the barn anyway," Venutha frowned.

"What?" Wren-at-Dawn put his hands on his hips.

"It's just too crowded," she shrugged. "Horses, dogs, and now cats and kittens. No, no, when I kiss, it's going to be while I'm dancing."

"Kiss?" Wren-at-Dawn blinked.

"Yeah," Venutha cocked her head. "What did you think I meant?"

Jeremy laughed and pulled her against his side. "Yep, my littermate was born in a barn, but won't be kissed in one."

"I'll be right back," Hreno dashed into the barn. There, she took a deep breath and smiled. The horses snorted and pranced nervously in their stalls. Momma Cat peered down at her from the loft, her ears flat against her head in alarm. Well-trained, Hreno immediately centered herself and peered into the dark corners trying to sense the danger.

From behind her, she heard a voice she had long thought she'd forgotten, "Hello, girly-girl."

"And then I minced the mushroom stems with the garlic and onions and slivered three small potatoes," Bunny's voice twittered from the kitchen.

"It's Ok, Bunny. I don't need to know everything," Mitchell tried to interrupt. "I just said it smelled good."

"It is good. It will be good!" Bunny grinned as the three dragoneers came through the door. "Look, Priest Mitchell and Shadoweave have come to eat with us!"

"Shadoweave?" Wren-at-Dawn repeated.

Bunny nodded enthusiastically.

"Ya'll have a seat after you wash up. There's plenty for everyone." Debbie put hot rolls on the table.

"It's Bunny's new name for me. I quite like it," Shadow allowed Mitchell to help her into a cane-bottomed chair.

"Go wash!" Debbie shushed them back into the hall. "Where's Hreno?"

"She's in the barn checking on the kittens."

"Well, I hope she hurries. Bunny got the idea of this soup from her."

Mitchell grunted.

"Ow," Debbie pressed her hand against her left shoulder.

At the stove, the ladle clattered to the floor as Bunny covered his face in fear.

"What is it?" Jeremy growled.

Wren-at-Dawn stated, "The door opens; the dance begins."

There was a small, abandoned army base thirty-seven miles north of where the tracking device showed Stelt to be. It had taken some doing, but her training in the IIA had been more than sufficient to make all the arrangements. From her camp in

166

Montana, she'd transported her 498 soldiers in semi-trailers and arrived during the night. Eight hours of sleep each night and two days of maneuvers had her soldiers stoked and ready to fight. The Corvette crept along the old Georgia road as dusk fell; the proximity beep becoming stronger and stronger as Cortez's car neared the farm.

"It's coming from over there, about a mile through those fields."

Cortez stopped the car and she and her lieutenant got out. "Open a door. We'll march them across the fields until we flush Stelt out of his hole."

"How do you know which direction to move us?"

She scoffed and pointed up. "That, my dear man, is a dragon."

"On my world, it's called a caveworm – stupid and not worth the eating unless it is very young. Why bother with the creature?"

"Because, on my world, dragons don't exist."

He squinted at her but said nothing.

"So, you open the door, my men march that way, we surround and capture Stelt. And then we'll take his girl."

"He'll kill her before he'll let her turn."

"Bjorak, you're a broken record."

"I'm what?"

"Open the damn door."

"Bless this food to our use and us to Thy service. Make us ever mindful –" Atticus groaned.

"A door, and it's close!" Natalie jumped up from the table. The claxon alarm set up by Tyler years ago went off.

The McAfee twins were louder than the claxon as Patsy kissed her husband good-by. He held his cell phone to his ear and cranked up the truck.

"Hreno's in the barn!" Jeremy bolted toward the back door but Wren-at-Dawn grabbed his arm.

"I'll come with you."

"Bring her back here, we'll hide in the basement," Debbie commanded.

"We're no safer in the basement than we'd be in the barn," Jeremy shouted over his shoulder and the boys ran into the yard.

"The orchard!" Venutha snatched Bunny into her arms. "Follow me! Hreno and I wove a holy place in the orchard – it's where the dragons could lay their eggs."

"The dark soldiers are coming from across the fields from the east," Mitchell placed Shadow's hand on his arm.

Debbie held the door as they all dashed out of the house.

"Hreno!" Jeremy shouted. He and Wren-at-Dawn reached the barn door at the same time.

They heard her voice, "Hide. Father, hide. They'll kill you sure as look at you."

"I'll not leave you. You're littermates have no reason to kill me. Not now."

"You killed Lanza."

Jeremy yelped as power surged through Wren-at-Dawn. The door flew open.

"I did not kill the Singer. I avenged her death."

Jeremy grabbed Wren-at-Dawn's arm. Cautiously, they entered the barn.

Stelt turned to face them. "Here I stand. This I swear. I was once like you. I loved a woman. I served the Light. When the Dark soldiers came to our village, my wife was no older than Venutha is now. They feasted on her." His voice was trembling. "The only way to keep Hreno alive was to turn to despair. To join them. To keep her safe. Here I stand. As this child's father, I swear to you I did not kill your woman, Horseman of Atticus. I avenged her death."

He flung a small shriveled lump at the floor between them. "He took her voice; I took his tongue."

"And then you led dark soldiers to us," Wren-at-Dawn growled.

"No, that's not my doing." Stelt bowed his head and then squared his shoulders, "But it is tied to me being here. Before the Assassin died, he told me that our Strategia Oscura Cortez placed a charm inside my body, so that she can know where I am at all times. I thought I would have more time, after I killed the Assassin. Time to say goodbye."

A dragon belched fire across the fields. Men screamed in agony. Commands were shouted from three directions. Inside the barn, horses whinnied and stomped against the stalls.

"Open a portal, Horseman. Take my girly-girl to safety."

"No, you can't go through a portal! You'll die."

"We can't leave the others," Jeremy's voice cracked.

"Horseman," Stelt began again.

Hreno shrieked and fell. An arrow stuck out of her side. Sounds of battle crept closer to the barn.

Stelt picked up his daughter. "Lead us, Animal Healer."

"Wait!" Jeremy shouted out a command and the horses dashed out toward the field, ready to fight. "This way!" he shouted to the humans.

The men ran into the grove as dragons rained spears of fire onto dark soldiers. Summer crops of tomatoes and vines ignited and dusk took on a golden hue.

"John!" Venutha cried in surprise. "It's John and he's carrying Hreno!"

Debbie looked to where Venutha was pointing and saw a coyote looping along toward her. The coyote had a girl on his back. Then the light shimmered and she saw three men running into the grove. Behind them, a dozen dark soldiers caught sight of them and jeered.

The three stopped right at the edge of the grove.

Venutha held out her hands, "Stop! John, this is holy ground. You can't come in here."

"I'll take Hreno." Jeremy reached for her.

"No," the father shook his head. Slowly, he stepped into the grove. If he felt pain for being on holy ground, it did not show on his face. As a matter of fact, his face began to glow.

When they were in the center, Stelt spoke again. "Now, Horseman, open a portal and take my child to safety."

"You can't! John can't go through a portal," Venutha argued.

"Ask me." Stelt faced Mitchel. "Ask me, Priest."

"Whom do you serve?"

Stelt began to cry, "I serve the Light, the Bringers of Light, and the Light Eternal."

Hreno whimpered.

"Now, hurry. I've never heard of six weaves being in the same place. I can't imagine the things a strategia obscura wouldn't do to own you all."

Bunny clung to Debbie's skirt, "He's a talking coyote, Grandmother Spider."

"I see it," she pushed him behind her protectively. "I see you, Coyote."

"Yes," John squinted at her. "I see that you do. But, I will go through the portal with you. This flesh has done dark things and must pay for those sins. But once free of the flesh, my soul," he bent his head down and kissed Hreno's forehead, "Yes girly girl, my soul will fly with you."

As Debbie watched, Mitchell embraced Shadow and they were engulfed in a brilliant white cloud. Inside the cloud, Debbie could see, not two teens, but a giant white buffalo and a calf-maiden. "Come," she heard a voice command.

Bunny took her hand, Wren-at-Dawn grabbed Venutha's elbow, Jeremy stood next to Stelt and reached for Hreno. "You don't have to go through, John."

"Yes. Yes, I do, Healer." The redeemed man smiled and stepped into the light.

On the other side, Jeremy caught Hreno before she fell. On Earth, a pile of bones clattered to the ground in a cloud of dust.

"Run!" Bunny yelled. Behind them, hoards of dark soldiers fought their way through horses and townspeople to get to the weaves.

They stepped from chaos through to silence. The smell of mint and fresh mown hay carried a warm dawn breeze toward them. Behind them, the White Buffalo and the Calf-Maiden embraced again and the white cloud disappeared.

"Where did they go? Where is Priest Mitchell and Shadoweave?" Bunny asked.

"Venutha, I need bandages. I've got to get the arrow out."

"We need to find shelter. If a Dark Lord is nearby, he'll grow curious." Venutha stepped out of her broomstick skirt and began ripping it into strips.

"That was a powerful weave," Wren-at-Dawn's eyes scoured the country side. "Too powerful."

"I can't see their weave anymore. The Priest and Shadoweave – they've gone," Bunny sobbed.

"Gone? Why do you keep saying that? Gone where?" Debbie picked up the boy.

"They're just gone."

"A portal." Wren-at-Dawn shook from head to toe but sounded calm. "They've become a portal."

"Not just opened one," Bunny whispered from the safety of Debbie's arms. "Become one."

Taralyn and Doug launched themselves from the vans and took positions around the Waystation. The dark soldiers were everywhere. Taralyn saw Doug fighting hand-to-hand with three dark soldiers. When he fell, she screamed and put out her hand. The ring on her finger, the ring that had slipped itself onto her finger years ago when they were too late to save the jewelers, burned like fire and a shard of white lightening erupted from it. What used to be fields of soybeans burst into flames. Taralyn trembled and began to run toward where she'd last seen her husband.

Morgan was blinded by two lights, one to his left where, unbeknownst to him, Taralyn's ring had just blasted the soybean field, and one to his right, as the largest portal he had ever seen was opened in the grove beyond the fields. The dark soldiers shrank away from its purity and in that moment, he called out, "Cortez! Lay down your weapons. Surrender!"

The woman who had once shared his bed but never his heart threw her head back and cackled. "Or what?"

"You're under arrest, Captain. Lay down your weapons and surrender your army to me."

She paused as if considering his command. Then she grinned as a dark door shadowed the night behind her. "Good night, sweetie." She blew Morgan a kiss and stepped backwards into nothingness.

"What do you mean, there's no residual weave?" Atticus growled at the elders.

Rawan answered, "There are very few prayer warriors here who are strong enough to even see a weave, but they say there is nothing here."

"We all saw the portal. It was the strongest thing I've ever seen," Sara insisted. "My son is out there somewhere – "

"Yes, Mitchell is out there, along with anyone else who could see, let alone recreate a weave." Rawan crossed her arms angrily.

"That was stupid," Le'Vander mumbled to Patsy. "Why'd we keep all our eggs in one basket?"

Morgan overheard him and blinked.

"Wherever they are, they're together and safe," Atticus assured them. "They'll come back the same way they left – in a portal."

Morgan saw Gwen's head come up. She looked at her husband, hearing the lie in his words as only a wife could. She glanced at the elders and then looked down; keeping her thoughts to herself.

"So, where do we stand on the Waystation?" Atticus cleared his throat, "Morgan, where do we stand on the Station?"

The general blinked again, feeling sick. "The dark soldiers Cortez left behind are dead. We've disposed of the bodies using four monasteries from three different states –and yes," he held up a hand. "They'll be given decent burials. I don't know how many she took back with her, but to my reckoning, she had barely three dozen left out of hundreds."

"Do you know where she went?" Larry asked.

Morgan gritted his teeth but replied cautiously, "The weave is there, but as Rawan pointed out, the only ones who could read the weave," he glanced at Le'Vander, "are gone."

Le'Vander blinked once and then nodded at his friend.

"Well, there's no way to get the dragons back to their world without the weaves," Le'Vander rode beside Morgan as they watched the sun become eclipsed by a pregnant dragon. Taralyn, Doug, Chinan, Ben and Pierre rode with them.

"How many eggs does a dragon lay?" Morgan asked.

"About a dozen, or so Otka says." Pierre plucked a tomato from a vine and polished it against his shirt."She'll be along soon and I don't have to tell you – she's furious about this. Ain't no way this farm will be big enough to raise a dozen dragons in, let alone the next batch, which by Otka's counting might could be in twelve months."

"I'm surprised the Angel of the Lord didn't warn Atticus about this," Morgan lowered his voice although there was no one else around. "About putting all of our eggs in one basket."

Le'Vander nodded, accepting whatever the cost for this breach of loyalty to Atticus. "That's not all the Angel of the Lord has been silent about."

"Like what?"

Le'Vander rubbed his nose and nodded at Taralyn.

"Taralyn, Staff of Atticus, I heard a new weapon was used during the battle. It was not from the dragons, though, am I right?" Chinan asked.

Taralyn took a deep breath, "We're almost there. Wait."

"I warned you, all those years ago when we were on the bluestone shelf. I warned you."

"Just wait," Taralyn refused to look at the horseman.

A thin creek ran through a grove of peaches and pecan trees. A woman was silhouetted by the small campfire as she moved around it. The horsemen dismounted and tied their horses to the trees. The woman stopped, her back to the flames. They approached her.

Morgan snorted. "Good evening, Gwen."

"Chinan, once we are seated, would you weave a silencer around us?"

"Yes, Wife-Staff of Atticus." The young man bowed.

"You know of Sanchor? And how the Angel of the Lord brought me to Atticus here?"

They nodded and silently let her find her way to the telling of this tale.

"Sanchor gave me this ring." She held her left hand up and the gems sparkled in the firelight. "It used to be so huge, I had to carry it around my neck on a chord. I hid it under my bed and then when we moved to the new parsonage in the Refuge, I put it inside the safe. It stayed there until Taralyn came to see me two nights ago. I put it on that night. Now, it's so tight, I can't get it off my thumb. But it's the same ring."

Ben pointed, "That Dark Lord who kidnapped the Crystal Lake children had one of those, too. He killed Rutgar with it."

Gwen nodded and then looked at Taralyn. The young mother shifted on the log and then held up her hand. A band of silver encircled her right index finger, gems sparkling around it. "The jewelers we couldn't save on Ricean's world hid a bag of these before they were slaughtered. I found them. This one found its way onto my finger when I put my hand in the bag. I've never been able to take it off, but I didn't think about it until three nights ago."

"That's what you used? That's what split a hole into the sky the night of the battle?" Morgan squinted at the light that was building on her hand.

She nodded. "I didn't mean to. I just put my hand out to stop them."

"And you did," Doug leaned against her shoulder.

Chinan cleared his throat.

"Go on, boy, what do you have to say?" Pierre whispered.

"The ring cannot come off, because it is now part of you."

"You've seen them before?" Le'Vander asked.

"Never. But I have heard tales, legends. On my home world, rings were forged and worn by Stone Singers until – long before the war came to us. Hundreds of years ago, Stone Singers became so powerful, they were all put to death. Anyone who had the ability to hear the stones sing was put to death, no matter how old or young. Eventually, no more Stone Singers arose, and my world was left defenseless when the Darkness fell. What you have, what you are now, Taralyn, is more power than even Priest Mitchel and Shadow could hold."

"I gave him one. I gave Mitchel one of the rings. I was hoping he could use it to keep from going wild."

"And now he and Shadow have lost themselves. They are what forms the portals." Chinan took a step backward and his silencer shimmered.

Le'Vander blinked as his voice caught, "Can't we get them back? Is that what you meant, Morgan, about the Angel not knowing about Mitchel and Shadow being lost?"

"Atticus has been praying for days, but he says the Angel hasn't spoken to him since the Battle of Crystal Lake," Gwen twirled the ring, pursing her lips.

"It's more than that," Ben added. "Pierre, you need to tell them."

They looked at the Cajun.

"You know I can see things."

The group nodded.

"I see some things, I don't see others. Up until three days ago, I seen Hreno and Jeremy and their children. I seen Morgan and Miss Debbie and well, that's saying a lot there since you've never said nothing to her yet. I seen Bunny and his wives and all their children and grandchildren, and then some! And you think I call Venutha queen just because of her regal ways, you'd be wrong. I see Queen Venutha. She's a queen and therefore I call her that."

Le'Vander smiled, "I ain't bowing to her, but I can see her as royalty myself."

Morgan took a deep breath, "What about Mitchell and Shadow?"

Pierre rubbed his cheeks; Ben recognized his friend's stalling gesture. "Well, the priest, I only been able to see a bright light around him, when he don't know I'm looking. And the girl, I ain't never seen anything about her. Sometimes I do see, sometimes I don't."

"But now, what do you see? Now, three days later?" Morgan asked.

"I don't see nothing. They are not there. All their futures, all their lives; it's as if someone walled them up inside a tower and all I see is sparkly stones."

A dragon screamed out a joyful chortle as it flew overhead, startling the people by the fire.

"Those stones that I see in my mind's eye," Pierre touched his nose. "They look mighty like what you got on your fingers, ladies."

"So, they might be safe," Ben added.

"What else can the rings do?" Morgan leaned closer.

"They choose their owners, like horses choose their riders." Chinan was sweating.

"So why didn't the Angel tell Atticus about this when I first got here? I had it with me then."

"That would be the same time you were pregnant, and Atticus didn't know?" Taralyn smirked.

"So, the Angel doesn't tell Atticus everything. That sounds like those angels in the Bible," Le'Vander posed.

"Maybe the Angel doesn't know everything," Doug suggested.

"Or he's not an angel," Taralyn added.

"What else can the rings do?" Morgan repeated firmly.

Taralyn met his gaze, then held out the burlap bag. Morgan put his hand inside and grunted. He blinked and snorted, then pulled his hand out. A heavy garnet-like stone encrusted a thick braided silver band on his middle finger.

Taralyn held the bag out to Le'Vander. The handyman rubbed his eyes and drew in a deep breath. He began to sit back but plunged his hand into the bag before he could change his mind. He pulled out his hand that now wore a thin silver band with a chunk of amethyst embedded onto it. "Jesus wept," he whispered.

Ben and Pierre looked at each other and put their hands in at the same time. Cabochon ruby encrusted Pierre's silver band, cabochon emerald encrusted Ben's.

Taralyn held the bag out to Chinan who said, "Doug, Weapon of Atticus, has more rank than I."

Doug shook his head and frowned, "It wouldn't, none of them would stay on my fingers. They didn't choose me."

"Why not?" Le'Vander asked.

"I do not know." Chinan looked away.

"Boy?" Pierre whispered.

"The ring chooses it's wearer. It's not a matter of you wanting it, it matters that the ring wants you."

"Well," Doug sniffed, "Clear as anything else has been these last few years. Put your hand in the bag."

Chinan jumped backward and the silencer snapped off. "No."

Gwen took him gently by the elbows and looked up into his face. "If we are to hold back the dark, we must know how to use these weapons. You are the only person we can trust who knows the legends from the other worlds."

"The worlds that lost to the Darkness," Pierre added.

"The line between light and dark is too thin once one wears a ring."

Morgan pointed at Taralyn, "Her shard of light was pure white, the dark lord's was pure black. There was no gray in either."

Chinan hung his head, "Perhaps because Taralyn is pure light and the other one was pure darkness."

"And you are afraid," Ben led him to a possible conclusion, but the horseman vigorously shook his head.

"No, I am not afraid – I serve the light, the bringers of light, and the light eternal."

"I dropped the ring once, and you picked it up. You knew what it was then."

Chinan nodded but refused to look directly at Taralyn.

"Seems likely the ring done chose you, boy. Might as well accept it."

Chinan looked at Pierre, then took the bag. He closed his eyes and put in his hand. A pyramid of tiny pink and blue stones perched on a filigree silver band on his ring finger.

"That was the ring that fell out of the bag on the steeps. The one that chose you then."

"I know. I knew then."

"But why didn't you say anything?" Ben asked.

"I only want to be a horseman. Your horseman, Dad and Pop. That is all I want to be. And husband of Courtney. Now I cannot marry."

"What?" all the voices burst out.

"I train horses; I do not ride them into battle. But now, this ring, these rings, will ride US into battle."

"To hold back the dark," Doug said.

"To hold back the dark," Chinan affirmed, but tears streamed down his face.

"Atticus."

When Atticus opened his eyes to the voice, his bedroom was filled with light.

"Atticus, wake up."

Atticus sat up and rubbed his eyes. "Who are you?"

"You know me, Atticus. You must hurry."

"I know you? Who are you?" He tried to see into the white light.

"Atticus, I have known you all of my life. Trust me. Trust me now or it will all be for nothing. Get under your bed."

"Do what?"

"Get under your bed, Atticus."

Atticus shrugged and then stood up. As the six year old crawled under his bed, the window in his room shattered as gun fire riddled holes into where he had been sleeping.

ejr

Characters

Character	Age	Title	Spouse	Parent 1	Parent 2	Children
Andrew McAfee	4			Le'Vander	Patsy	
Atticus Jordan	45	Priest	Gwen			Natali, Easter Jordan, Rutger
Avery Ditka	37		Missy			Suzie, Beth
Baby Ben Feinstein	3			Benjamin	Joan	
Beatrice "Bea" Horne	76	Teacher				(Andrew)
Beaucephus McAfee	42					
Becky Leedy Iglesias	29		Gabriel	Debbie		Devin, Thomas
Benjamin Feinstein	45	Healer	Joan			Venusha, Dog Guards, Baby Ben
Beth Ditka	8			Avery	Missy	
Bunny	6	Weave				
Charity Jordan	3			Atticus	Gwen	
Chi Abubakar, MD	48	Healer	Visolela			Kayien
Chinan	28	Horseman				
Debbie Leedy	51	weave		Minister		Becky, Rachel, Miriam

Character	Age	Title	Spouse	Parent 1	Parent 2	Children
Devin Iglesias	10			Gabriel	Becky	
Doug Tompkins	33	Hand	Taralyn			
Easter Jordan	6			Gwen	Atticus	
Eduviges McGuinna	66	Music				
Elke Perkins	75	Staff		Rutger	Kaela	
Flowers-on-a-Vine-at-Midnight		Dragon	Scarlet-Sun-Rising-Across-the-Desert			
Foofaha "Jake"		Dog - schnauzer				
Gabriel Iglesias	30	Sheriff	Becky			Devin, Thomas
Gamga "Roland"		Dog - german shepherd				
Gugandeep		Dragon				
Gweneviere Hampt Jordan "Gwen"	43	Warrior	Atticus	Clive	Amanda	Natali, Easter Jordan, Rutger
Hreno	17	Weave		Pierre adpt	Stelt	
Isabel Cortez	42	Strategia Obscura				
Jeremy Dart	18	Healer				

Character	Age	Title	Spouse	Parent 1	Parent 2	Children
Joan Peters Feinstein	40		Ben			
Kayien Abubakar	8			Chi	Visolela	
Lanza	16	Music				
Larry Sveete	60	Finances	Sara			(nicholas), Mitchell, James, patrick, Simon, Thaddeus
Le'Vander McAfee	38	Weapons	Patsy	(Pearl McAfee)		
Levi McAfee	4			Le'Vander	Patsy	
Little Rutger Jordan	baby			Atticus	Gwen	
Magyar		Dog - pit bull				
Missy Forest Ditka	33		Avery	Morgan		Suzie, Beth
Mitchell Sveete	18	Prayer		Larry	Sara	
Morgan Forest	61	Weapons	(Annie)			Missy, Suz
Morning Dew		Horse				
Natalie Jordan	8			Gwen	Sanchor	
Ohamaha		Dog - labrador				
Otka Kinski	30	Dragoneer				

Character	Age	Title	Spouse	Parent 1	Parent 2	Children
Owawa	pup	Dog - mixed		Ohamaha	Gamga	
Patsy Weldon McAfee	38	Music	Le'Vander	(Peggy Weldon)		
Pearl McAfee	2			Le'Vander	Patsy	
Peggy McAfee	2			Le'Vander	Patsy	
Pierre Gilles	51	Horseman				Wren-at-Dawn, Horsemen
Rawan Collier	63	Healer				
Ricean Fogel	44	Sword	Tyler			Ormed
Rorah		Dog - cairn terrier				
Runs-at-Waters-Edge		Horse				
Samir Ahmadinaja	67	Acquisitions				
Sara Sveete	57	Staff	Larry			(Nicholas), Mitchell, James, Patrick, Simon, Thaddeus
Scarlet-Sun-Rising-Across-the-Desert		Dragon	Flowers-on-a-Vine-at-Midnight			

185

Character	Age	Title	Spouse	Parent 1	Parent 2	Children
Shadow	19	Weave				
Stelt "John Parker"	32	Redeemer				Hreno
Steve Ives	35		Suz			
Suz Forest Ives	31		Steve	Morgan		
Suzie Ditka	10			Avery	Missy	
Taralyn Fogel Tompkins	25	Staff	Doug Tompkins	Tyler	(Beth)	
Thomas Iglesias	12			Gabriel	Becky	
Tyler Fogel	51	Tech	Ricean			Taralyn Fogel
Venusha Feinstein	14	Animals		Ben adpt		
Visolela Abubakar	45	Acquisitions	Chi			Kayien
Wren-at-Dawn	19	Weave		Pierre adpt		
Zaris	67	Assassin				

*(deceased)

ABOUT THE AUTHOR

Evelyn Rainey has always loved to tell stories and help others understand. As such, she is a published author and educator. But she is also the caregiver of her mother, an herb and vegetable gardener, cat wrangler, and crochet artist. She is in the process of obtaining her Masters in Biblical Studies.

After 38 years in education, Evelyn retired, having earned degrees and certificates in Early Childhood Education, Elementary Education, Gifted Education, Integrated Middle School Curriculum, English for Speakers of Other Languages, and Journalism. She also taught all grade levels from Kindergarten through Adult and at many different facilities, including jails and teen pregnancy centers.

Evelyn has had several books published including science fiction, fantasy, historical fiction, new age urban fantasy, and children's books. She currently has a list of dozens of new projects she plans to have published over the next few decades. She has facilitated writer groups and been guest speaker and guest author at writer conferences and conventions throughout the southeast US.

Her love of teaching has expanded into videos for book trailers, crochet lessons, and Bible studies. Her love of writing has expanded into managing ShelteringTree.Earth, LLC Publishing.

She loves corresponding with readers and authors and is available for conferences and other book events in person or through online meetings. Her website and contact information can be found on EvelynRainey.com .

TO HOLD BACK THE DARK

Discussion Guide For Book Clubs, Journaling,
Or Personal Contemplation

1. If you had to choose between killing someone swiftly and with mercy or torturing them until they give up, which would you choose?
2. The Bible teaches that the sins of the father are visited on his children for generations to come (*Yet he does not leave the guilty unpunished; he punishes the children and their children for the sin of the parents to the third and fourth generation.* Exodus 34:7). What do you think about that?
3. Is Atticus the good guy or the bad guy in this book? Why?
4. Describe the similarities and differences between Stelt "John Parker" and Zaris the Assassin. Identify each one's redeeming feature and damning trait.
5. Dragon poetry is quite rich. Compose a dragon poem for your loved one.
6. Play matchmaker. Who do you think will become romantically involved in the next books? Who do you think will marry? Why?
7. Why do you think Atticus placed all the Weaves at the Waystation?
8. Who do you think is the Angel of the Lord in this series?
9. The idea that praying with Atticus changes people's

minds – making the able to breathe on other planets and eat the native foods there and become prolific – is brought up several times in this book. How did that make you feel?

10. If you could have one of the skills presented in this series, what would it be? Why? Is it something you could develop and learn?

11. What do you know about the power of gemstones? What is your favorite gem and why? If you had a ring of power, describe it, including what it looks like and how it works.

12. Where do you think the Weaves went?

13. Would you want to live in The Refuge? Why or why not? Are there places similar to the Refuge on Earth today or were there in the past?

14. Procreation is a prominent theme in this book. It was also the first commandment in the Bible (*As for you, be fruitful and increase in number; multiply on the earth and increase upon it.* Genesis 9:7) and was the pivotal selling point of the contract between God and Abrahman (*I will surely bless you and make your descendants as numerous as the stars in the sky and as the sand on the seashore. Your descendants will take possession of the cities of their enemies*, Genesis 22:17) What is your opinion about population, and family-size? Did you decide to limit the number of your children? Why or why not?

15. The Waystation has been used to name a place of refuge found along the path of a long and often dangerous journey. What do you think the purpose of the waystation in this book is?

16. There are many connections in this book to Native American spiritual stories, one of which is the trickster coyote. Who do you know that has the same characteristics of Coyote? Discuss how you are related and how you feel about that person.
17. Knitting is an ancient art; crochet is only 500 years old. Do you crochet, knit, or pursue another form of fabric art? Do you embue your creations with power? Why or why not?
18. What is your opinion of serial killers? How should they be treated? Is there redemption for them? Will they still, like Stelt, have to face the physical consequences of their sins?
19. Of the characters in this book, who has suffered the most? Achieved the most? Changed the most?
20. Of the characters in this series so far, who has suffered the most? Achieved the most? Changed the most?

TO HOLD BACK THE DARK

We are an exclusive traditional publishing house.

Our readers, once they finish one of our books, will be able to get up and face the world wiser, stronger, centered, and with the assurance that we are not alone: we are all a part of the Sheltering Tree on Earth.

If you as a writer feel that same calling, please refer to

ShelteringTree.Earth/writer-guidelines

www.ingramcontent.com/pod-product-compliance
Lightning Source LLC
Chambersburg PA
CBHW060643260626
47161CB00008B/2974